The Absen

# THE ABSENT FATHER

Corey G. Carolina

Printed in the United States of America First Printing, 2016

ISBN 978-0-9975092-0-5

Rise and Develop Publishing

3642 South 106th East Place
Tulsa, OK 74146

Visit-www.CoreyCarolina.com
Email-corey@coreycarolina.com

The Absent Father

THE ABSENT
FATHER

# Table of Contents

# Dedication

This book is dedicated to all the boy and girls who have had to grow up without their father in their lives. I also dedicate this book to my father who was not there for me as much as I hoped when I was growing up but has made an effort to build a better relationship with me. This book would not have been able to be written if it wasn't for my great mother who raised my brother and I while working 12-16 hour days. It took a village to raise me so I want to also dedicate this book to all the uncles, step-fathers, grand-parents, aunts, brothers, cousins, and community leaders who are involved in the lives of children to help ensure that they will have a meaningful life and become the best adults possible.

You will hear about my uncle Sylvester later in this book. He was my main male father figure while growing up and to this day is the only man I say I love you to on a regular basis. To the single mother and fathers, I salute you. To the fathers and mothers who are in their children's lives, I take my hat off to you. Finally I dedicate this book to my wife and wonderful blessings Elle and Ellington. They are my WHY. They are the reason why I push forward to try to be successful. I want to be a great role model for my children but I find sometimes they teach me about life.

# Intro

My name is Corey Carolina, a 27-year-old man when I started writing this book, and a 35-year-old man when I finished it. As a child, I had an experience that is similar to so many other children and adults. I felt it was important to share my story, because so many young children never get to tell their stories, either because they have been silenced, or because they have buried their feelings deep within their souls.

*The Absent Father* is a story about my relationship, or lack thereof, with a man who is half responsible for my coming into this world. A relationship between a father and his son marks a special bond. If a young boy grows up without a key piece of the puzzle for development, he may have a disadvantage over a young boy brought up in a two-parent household.

It is my firm belief that a child is better off with both parents, but in truth, that does not happen regularly. I also believe a child is not doomed just because the father is not around. I was blessed to have a strong mother to raise me, since my father was not often around to help. A single mother has a unique situation because she has to be both the mother and father at the same time.

My single mother did a great job as the responsible figure in my life. Even though some may think a woman cannot teach a young boy how to be a man, thousands of women work hard to do just that. A woman may not know precisely how to be a man, but she does know what a good man looks, sounds, and acts like. She can also teach a young boy how to be responsible, take care of business, treat others with respect, and be an overall good person.

There are a variety of reasons why a father may not be around to help raise his child. It can be because the mother does not allow him to come around, or perhaps he has chosen not to be a part of the child's life. In many cases, the man is in prison, or he has another family to which he has chosen to devote his time and resources.

As a father myself, I have an even deeper appreciation for the hard work single mothers and fathers go through daily. I have two young children, with my wife, Qianna Carolina, and they all are my entire world. I cannot imagine not being in my children's lives. I refuse to ever be an absent father. I know how hurtful it was to me as a young boy, and even as an adult.

My mother raised my brother and me while working 16-hour days to keep food on the table and a roof over our heads. She was our provider and teacher. I told myself when I had children, I would always be there for them. I would always sacrifice everything I could to ensure they had a better life than I did, and that they were prepared to become successful adults. So many fathers feel the same way. They do not get enough credit for the men they have become and the way they are raising our future leaders. Unfortunately, there are far too many fathers who do not step up. I promised myself I would not be that way.

I was born in Tulsa, Oklahoma; I was the first-born of a 21-year-old woman. My brother was born later. My mother met my father while working at The Tulsa World. My father is very charming, as are all the men on his side of the family. I could see how my mother fell for him. He is an educated man with a degree in Sociology from The University of Tulsa.

I do not know the entire extent of their relationship, as is the case with most children, but I was born in 1981. I believe my father was initially around. I was introduced to his side of the family when I was about 6 months old. From what my mother tells me, his side of the family fell in love with me. I can see that's true because they are so supportive, even now.

The head of my father's family was my grandfather, David Carolina. He was a mechanic and an extremely charming and funny man. He was also the Mayor of the small town of Moffett, Oklahoma, just one mile west of Fort Smith, Arkansas. He passed away too soon and I think about him all the time. I truly miss him. My mother felt it was important that my brother and I know our father's side of the family.

Every summer, for about four years, my mother sent my brother and me down to Fort Smith, Arkansas, where my father lived. During those summers, I began to build a strong relationship with my grandfather and my uncle, Sylvester. Even though my brother and I were sent to visit our father, we seemed to spend more time with our grandfather and our uncle Sylvester.

My father is about 10 years older than my mother, and he had three other children before I was born. I mention the age difference because we sometimes think absent fathers are young, and just irresponsible but there are plenty of absent fathers who are not 15 or 16 years old. Even though my father was older, there was no guarantee that he would provide for his children.

I am so passionate about not being an absent father: first, because I cried myself to sleep so many times as a young boy, and second, because my wife and I lost four babies before we were blessed with our first child. I remember the first time we thought we were pregnant. We had been married for about a year when she took a pregnancy test and it turned out positive. We had been trying to have a baby since we got married, so we were excited about the news.

She scheduled an appointment with her doctor, and when he confirmed she was pregnant, I was on cloud nine. The doctor said some of my wife's tests looked troubling, so he wanted to keep an eye on her results to see if the baby was progressing as expected. When we went back in to meet with the doctor, he told us her progesterone levels were very low. He gave her an ultrasound, and he could not find a fetus. He told us she had a tubular pregnancy, which means the fetus was in the fallopian tube, and if we did not have a procedure to remove the fetus, her tube could burst, which could prevent her from having children in the future. We had to make the difficult decision to have the procedure.

After we tried unsuccessfully for almost another year to get pregnant, we decided to seek the advice of a fertility doctor. Our doctor was excellent, and she advised us to try in vitro fertilization, a process whereby the doctor retrieves mature eggs from the ovaries and fertilizes with sperm in a lab. We sat down with the financial counselor, so she could explain the cost of having the in vitro fertilization. She let us know the procedures were not covered under insurance, so we would have to come up with $13,000 within three weeks to start the process. We were initially in a panic because we knew we did not have the money, and the success rate was less than fifty percent, but we pulled the money together.

To start the in vitro fertilization process, we had to prepare my wife's body for retrieving her eggs. Each day, we had to use a needle to inject her with medicine to spark the ovulation process. This was a painful process for my wife, but she was so strong; she was dedicated to doing anything possible to have a baby. Ultimately, we ended up with three viable fertilized eggs. The doctor advised us she could use one, two, or three eggs to see if they would create an embryo. We decided to use all three eggs.

Over the next couple of weeks, we waited to see if our dream would come true. I remember the call I got from my wife as if it were yesterday. She called me, on my birthday, during lunch, while I was signing an agreement to rent a commercial kitchen to start making my wine jelly, Toasted. I missed her first call, so she sent me a text message to call her as soon as I could. When I called her, she said she had been to the doctor, and none of the Eggs had survived; we had lost all three. My world stopped. My babies were gone. Even though they were just in the embryo stage, I had a picture of them in my mind, and they were my babies. Now they were gone.

This was a difficult time in my marriage, because we had to consider what would happen if we could not conceive children. Privately, I wondered if our relationship would survive. We had lost our babies and $13,000, and I was so angry; I was even angry with God. I felt he was punishing me for some reason, and it was not fair. I wondered why other people, who didn't even want their children, were able to give birth so easily. How would I pay off the $11,000 loan I took out? How would I be supportive of my wife while I was still grieving? I apologized to God for being angry with him. I told him I understood things happen for a reason, and that I trusted he knew the best path for us.

We met with the fertility doctor again, and she said if we wanted to try the procedure again, she would give us a small discount. We were still going to have to come up with around $10,000, and we didn't have it. My wife and I decided to take a break from trying to get pregnant, so we could just get our heads together. We thought we would try in vitro fertilization one more time in a few months. But God works in mysterious ways, in his own time, and we got pregnant naturally the very next month after we lost our babies. Elle was born later that year.

# Chapter One

# What is an Absent Father?

I came up with the notion of an absent father because I felt if a man has a child, it is important for him to be involved in the life of that child. If he is not involved, he is an absent father. It is not enough to merely pay child support or to see the child on special occasions; a father must be a big part in the child's life. Too many children have to grow up in a single-mother household.

They do not have the opportunity to talk about things their fathers taught them, or about the birthdays they spent with their fathers. Too often, the men who are supposed to be there for the family are in jail, have given up all rights to their children have decided that they can't deal with the mother, or have rationalized that because their fathers were absent in their own lives, that's reason enough to avoid being a part of their children's lives.

Imagine a world where the mother and father can get along enough to raise their children. Imagine if more families were out in the park and playing together, rather than visiting the father in prison. This world needs present fathers. A father needs to be there to not only support his children, but also to support his wife or significant other. It may be difficult to raise a child, but just think how difficult it is to raise a child by yourself. I think if the roles were reversed and the fathers had to take care of the children for a month by themselves, they would have a different view on the importance of helping the mother raise the children.

Growing up to be a man is difficult. There are constant challenges that must be encountered each day. If a man decides to have sex with a woman, he and she must be prepared for the consequences. A few minutes of fun or a lapse in judgment can have huge ramifications, such as conceiving a child. Men must step up and take responsibility for the decisions they make. Women must hold these men accountable and also take responsibility for the decision they make. Being absent in a child's life is not fair to the child. He or she did not ask to be a part of any argument in which the parents may be involved. Children just want to grow up and enjoy being children. When a man abandons his family, his young son may be forced to become the man of the house. Young boys need to be taught how to be men, how to take care of business, how to appreciate women, and how to be positive driving forces in their communities.

Young girls should be taught how to handle themselves when dealing with young boys. They need to understand that no man defines them as women; this does not have to be a man's world, and no matter what, a woman should never allow a man to put his hands on her, or disrespect her as a woman. A mother can only teach so much. A father is needed to provide his input, so there is a balance with what the child learns.

Being an absent father may seem appealing to some boys or men. They may think they can go out and do what they want and there will be no repercussions for their actions. They may think the mothers love them so much that they will not ask for child support. But it is time for a change in the way we raise our children. In our past, the fathers were kings, scholars, teachers, thinkers, politicians, and leaders; as men, we must teach our children the importance of having a male involved in their lives. It is not just enough to be in the same room with your children; you must talk to them, teach them, and love them. Men must not be afraid to show affection to their children; this does not make them look less manly. It just teaches the children how they should love, not only their own children, but others as well.

The absent father is affecting families all across the world. As a father, I cannot see myself not being with my children almost every day, or speaking with them when I do not see them. My children keep me focused and they drive me to strive for success.

As a young African-American man, I face many unique challenges. For hundreds of years, there has been a systematic approach to keeping people who look like me as ignorant as possible. During the days of slavery, blacks were not permitted to learn how to write or spell. We were viewed as no better than oxen or other animals. We were not considered civilized humans, but rather property to be bought and sold at the snap of a finger. We were even enslaved by people who looked like us. We wore clothes that were handed down. We had no knowledge of the currency or capitalism. We had no wealth or education. All we had was our culture and history.

But even though we had our history, many of the slaves had either forgotten it or were not told about it. They did not know – and many of today's African-Americans do not know – that our ancestors were kings, educators, inventors, entrepreneurs, and scientists. Many people think slavery started when Africans were brought to America, but in fact, there were slaves in Egypt long before Africans were brought here. The people who built some of the monuments and the great wonders of the world were slaves. Their living conditions were poor. They were seen as expendable and not good for anything besides working and reproducing.

The mind of a slave is controlled by the failure to understand his own worth and value in the world. Some slaves realize their conditions are poor, but in their minds, they were better off than in other unknown conditions. They knew that for the most part, they could get food and some shelter. The horrendous conditions may be secondary to the security of a structured day.

African-American men statistically make up the highest population of absent fathers. During slavery, fathers were taken away from their families and forcefully sold to other slave owners. Those fathers may have never seen their wives and children again, so that meant the single mothers had to raise the children. The single mother is not a new concept; thousands of single mothers were created during slavery. Even now, there are thousands of single mothers, and they are still created by modern slavery. Being an absent father is like being a slave to the mindset that it is acceptable not to do everything possible to be in a child's life. Many men have allowed a slavery mindset to control their actions; they are languishing in prisons and jails right now as slaves in the justice system, and they have allowed themselves to create more single mothers to raise their children.

Our young men are growing up without fathers, and

they are lost. When I look into the eyes of my son, all I see is love and joy. These young boys have to learn how to love as men are supposed to love. A man loves by showing his family he is willing to do everything possible to ensure that his family members have food on the table and shelter over their heads.

Many young men turn to gangs because they want to belong and have a sense of brotherly love. I am sure most gang members would not confess to the need for brotherly or fatherly love as one of the reasons for joining the gangs. If the absent fathers do not come back into the lives of our young boys and girls, we will continue to allow our prison system to raise our children.

The prison guards will teach our sons and daughters how to be adults. Other prisoners will be their role models, and the cycle will continue with future generations. Our fathers must take an active role in ensuring that our youth learn how to be productive adults. This book is a collection of thoughts that have taken 35 years to write. The absent father is not just about men who are in prison or who have decided to leave the mothers of their children for a variety of reasons; this book is also about the fathers who live in the homes with their children, but do nothing to develop meaningful relationships with them.

A man can be an absent father even while he is present. This book will also define the present father – a father, stepfather, grandfather, uncle, friend, cousin, pastor, mentor, community leader, educator, counselor, caseworker, bus driver, etc., who does his best to be in the life of a child. A present father attends the child's special occasions or sporting events.

A present father teaches a child right from wrong, and ensures that the mother of that child is supported mentally and spiritually. Of course, the man must be physically there, for the child and the mother, but just because he is literally living with the mother does not make him a present father. So many great men are raising their children, or even raising children who are not their own, but they love them as if they were. We need more present fathers in our community. Being an absent or present father does not follow a certain race, religion, or sexual orientation. I hope this book allows me to continue the conversations about this topic, as I know so many people need this message.

# Chapter Two

# My Absent Father

From stories I heard about my father, he was a man with a great deal of talent. He was a great football player who attended the University of Tulsa on scholarship, and his photo is still posted in the athletic department there. He graduated with a bachelor's degree in Sociology. He was not only an exceptional athlete, but he had a great personality. He was a star athlete in basketball, football, and baseball, and he was a suave man who knew how to talk to people at any level and make them laugh. Women were attracted to his confidence and personality, so as with many men, he dealt with the temptations of women, drinking, and drugs. After getting involved with people who were going down the wrong road, my father began to follow them. He had children, and was not a major part in any of their lives. Unfortunately, he was an absent father.

My father is no different from other fathers who become absent. He was fortunate to have both parents in his life under the same roof until he was a toddler but because of certain circumstances, he was not raised after the age of five in a two-parent household. My father had the potential to do great things and make millions of dollars, but it did not work out that way, because he engaged in behavior and hung around people who did not have his best interests at heart. This happens so often in our lives.

We have people around us who we think are our friends, but later, we find out they were leading us in the wrong direction. My father had the world at the fingertips, so the question was not whether he could be successful, but how much success he would be able to achieve. He could have changed so many lives for the better. He could have had scholarships established in his name to ensure that children from disadvantaged situations had a chance to go to college. He could have done anything.

My mother told me my father was a great person when they were young. She fell in love with him and wanted to spend the rest of her life with him. Indeed, I can tell that she still loves him and wants the best for him. Many relationships end even when the couple still loves each other. Some people are better off separated instead of maintaining an intimate relationship, and that is the case for my parents.

I do not remember very many interactions between my mother and father, but the ones I do remember suggest they always loved each other. I never remember my parents arguing in front of me. I am sure they had their share of problems, but they never let it spill over for their children to see. I appreciate them for that.

I had complex feelings about my absent father while I was growing up. Although you might know you are supposed to "love" your father, you cannot force yourself to love him. My father had the perfect opportunity to raise his sons in his image of greatness, but he instead chose to have a hands-off approach to parenting. Thousands of young boys and girls live in this same situation.

I was fortunate that my father was not abusive. I only remember one time when he had to discipline me. When my brother and I were sent to stay with him during the summer, we went to my grandfather's house frequently. On this occasion, my brother and I were not replying back to my grandfather with the respectful, "Yes sir, no sir." That was a major issue, for both my grandfather and my father. My father came home from work and made me go out to pick out a switch for him to discipline me with.

Oddly, I felt like I was making my first adult decision. If I got a switch that was too green, it would wrap around my leg and hurt even worse, but if I got a twig that was dead, it would break when I was hit with it. Of course, I decided to go with the dead switch. I took it to my father and he just looked at me. He ended up going to get a different switch, much to my dismay. Needless to say, I still say, "yes sir, no sir" to as many people as possible on a daily basis.

As I have grown into an adult, I still wonder what caused my father to become an absent father. I initially felt something was wrong with me, and that I had somehow pushed my father away. I became convinced I was not good enough to be in his life. I frequently asked myself if he really was my father, because I felt he should be excited to have children. My father never showed me he was proud of me while I was growing up. I never remember him calling to ask how my grades were, or to congratulate me on winning awards.

I was so proud to be Student of the Month in elementary school. I felt I was making my mother proud, but where was my father? He was not there. It wasn't because he was in prison, or that he had passed away. He just wasn't there. As an adult, I still remember the important times when I needed my father, but he wasn't around. That's why I urge today's fathers to always attend the important events in their children's lives.

If your child is having a difficult time reading, or in

any other area in school, it is your responsibility to do everything possible to help her or him to improve. My father did not even know I was being bullied in elementary school, and since I never had a conversation with him about it, he could not give me advice on what to do. I could have used my father in that situation as well.

I am sure my father wondered how to build a relationship with me, his first-born son, since he was not heavily involved in raising me. I can only imagine what he thought would happen when I became an adult. I know as a father now that I would hate for my children not to have a good relationship with me, as they became adults. I cannot imagine not spending holidays with my children, or helping them through any difficulties they encounter. I can only hope my father thought about the fact that he was not in my life, and how that would affect me as a child and on into adulthood. My heart hopes he did think about these things, but my mind tells me he probably did not.

A man whom I was supposed to love, seek guidance from, and learn how to be a man from was not interested in how I turned out. At least, this is what I thought while growing up. He was absent, so I could not build the relationship I longed for with him. All I wanted to do was make him proud of me. As an adult, I now know I have made him proud. He has told me this many times.

My brothers and sisters were not fortunate enough to have him around, either, and it is sad that they had to deal with the same issues I faced. I have also spoken with so many people who have lived with the reality of an absent father, and we all seem to have a similar yearning for a better relationship with our fathers while we were growing up, and we all looked forward to a day when we could make that happen.

My father has the ability, as do most fathers, to rebuild strained relationships. But first, the father must want to build that relationship. He must admit to being a huge part of the problem, and actually acknowledge the hurt and pain he helped create for his children. But men are prideful, and it is hard for some of them to admit wrongdoing. Men need to look their children in the eyes and beg their forgiveness, and ask how they can start to build relationships with them. It can start with a phone conversation, a text message, a written letter or email.

It is not easy to start the conversation and to ask for forgiveness, but it is so rewarding as a child to know your father cares enough to admit his shortcomings. We, as children, are willing to move forward, but it is not easy.

Mothers can help with this process by offering themselves as a "middle ground" to foster the flow of communication between the child and the absent father. If the father and mother do not have a good relationship, it may be necessary to bring in someone who is familiar with both parents, such as a mother, brother, grandparent or father. There's nothing wrong with involving the man's family, because the most important consideration should be helping the children and their father build a relationship.

There are times when a relationship with the father is not possible because the man is simply a deadbeat, but the children should nevertheless have the opportunity to get to know their father's side of the family. The absent father may stay absent by his own wishes, but his mother, father, brother, uncle, and other family members deserve to have a connection with a blood relative. I did not have a relationship with my father growing up, but I was close to his siblings and his father. Although he was absent, his family was present. I thank my mother for not being afraid or too vindictive to allow my brother and me to build relationships with my father's side of the family. That decision turned out to be a key factor in allowing me to have the most important father figure in my life: my uncle Sylvester.

# Chapter Three

## The Child of an Absent Father

I was born to my mother and father in Tulsa, Oklahoma– a medium-sized city with a population of a little over 300,000 people. It is home for me. I enjoy the cold winters and the hot summers. Oklahoma is in what is known as the "Bible belt," and we have our share of problems, such as racial inequality, crime, and the lack of a strong education system. Our community is in some respects still segregated. We have a certain part of town each race calls home. You rarely see a focus on getting everyone together from all walks of life to discuss differences and to embrace one another. We are in a city that is historic in nature. Oklahoma is known for one of the worse events on United States soil; The Tulsa Race Riots. This tragedy crushed a race of African-Americans for generations. Over 300 black-owned businesses were burned and destroyed.

When I look back on my childhood and try to conjure up memories of my father, I can only recall limited episodes with him. I remember idolizing him as a young boy, because he was tall and he loved sports. He was my father, after all, and I told myself I would grow up big and strong just like him. I wanted to play basketball and football, just like my father. When I saw him interact with people; he was so cool, and people always smiled around him. He was the pride of the family, and that is what I wanted to be when I grew up.

My father knew how to talk to people, and had a promising career in football, but he was unable to capitalize on all his talent and skills. People wanted to know him and they loved having him around. He was supposed to be the anchor of the family, because he was the one going to college and who had the promising future. But my father chose to stay in the streets and do drugs. He could have played professional football, but he decided to join a newly formed semi-pro football league instead. The league eventually folded, and so did my father's dreams. I was the first of two boys my mother and father had together, and my father had three other children before I was born.

I was a normal young boy, full of life and very energetic. For some reason, I loved to wear old tattered clothes. I always found a favorite shirt and jeans and wore them almost every day. My elementary school girlfriend once asked me why I was wearing the same clothes over and over again.

I believe I got my charisma and charm from my father. My parents separated when I was young, but not before another little one came along. The birth of my little brother may have been one of the biggest blessings in my life. I adored my little brother. I remember asking my mother for a kid brother toy, My Buddy, and a few months later, I had a little brother. It was not what I was looking for, but I was so happy to be a big brother. I promised myself I would always take care of my brother. I felt that he was my responsibility.

As a child, I had a hard time identifying with my father. I knew he was my father, but I never felt he was approachable. We did not engage in the normal father-son activities like shooting hoops, throwing the football around, or playing catch with the baseball. I always thought a father was supposed to teach you how to do "guy things" like hunt, work on cars, play cards, or fish. I always felt strange because I only got to see those things on television. I told myself when I grew up, I would teach my boy how to be a man.

My father was a charismatic person and well known. After graduating from college and working a bit in Tulsa, he moved back to Arkansas, and my mother decided to move to Fort Smith, Arkansas, to be with him. My mother was loyal, and she wanted to make things work with my father. She loved him and wanted him to be with his boys.

To me, Fort Smith was a town similar to Tulsa with a diverse group of people. There were nice houses and there were houses in bad shape.

I do not have many good memories of those years. The kids I was around did not want to be kids; they wanted to be adults and do adult things. I was used to joking around and being silly, but these kids were trying to act older and run in the streets. It was a culture shock for me, and I did not want to get in trouble. I was afraid I would get caught up in the wrong place and get shot, beaten up, or kidnapped. I guess you can say I was a cautious child.

I remember my first fight with a local "tough kid." My brother and I were playing outside with some of our friends, and a group of youngsters approached us. This particular kid called my brother a "bitch". That was the first time I had to make a decision to fight or turn the other cheek. I said to the kid, "Don't talk to my brother like that." He challenged me: "What are you going to do?" I told him I would not let him talk to my brother like that. I was his big brother, after all, and it was my job to defend him. I do not think I really understood the situation, because I had never been in one like it before. I thought the bully would just back down and we would not have to fight. I intuitively knew if I backed down, the kid would think it was OK to talk to my brother like that. I said to him, "Well, you have to hit me." So he did; he punched me in the face, and we tussled for a bit, until the other kids separated us.

I walked back home, with my brother, and my face was swollen. I walked into our home and my mom asked, "What is wrong with you?" She saw my face and got very upset, until I explained the situation. She did not want me fighting, but she understood I had to protect my brother. That was my first chance to stand up for something, and I did. I look back on that altercation and realize it prepared me for the future. I do not advocate fighting, but I do feel you must fight for what you feel is right.

We stayed in Arkansas for four years, and then our mother decided to move back to Tulsa to get away from our father. Even so, she always wanted my brother and me to have a relationship with him. Each summer, she sent us to Arkansas to stay with our father, but still, I felt like he was a stranger, because I do not remember spending time with him.

While in Arkansas, I deliberately started to distance myself from my father. When he went to work, he either forgot to leave food for us on some days, or he just did not care what we ate. We had to fend for ourselves and find something around the house to eat. I was old enough to take care of my brother and I was used to it, since we were latchkey kids back home. Most of the time, we had to call our uncle, Sylvester, to pick us up and take us to get something to eat. I know he did not have to do that, but he never complained. He told us we were family, and family members take care of one another.

We spent most evenings with our uncle and grandfather, and then he took us back home. That's how I was able to make an emotional contact with important male figures in my life. I saw two men, though they were not my father, showing my brother and me more love than our own father did. That made me simultaneously happy and sad.

The man who was supposed to teach me how to be a man, how to ask a young lady out on a date, how to make sure my finances were in order, and how to take care of business was just a warm body, who did not know how to communicate with his young boys. I felt as if I was not important to him and he was only dealing with me because he was forced to do so. When I tried to talk to him, I felt like I was bothering him. I only remember one sit-down conversation my father and I ever had.

Another significant reason I drew away from my father was the life he chose to live. He made decisions that were not positive, such as being addicted to drugs. Imagine this story that a young man never told my mother about. This young man riding in the car with his father and his friends; they pulled up to a man and he witnessed his father purchasing drugs. There were a lot of people around, and they looked like unsavory characters. The young man was just 8 years old when this happened, but he could remember that incident in great detail, even down to the area where it happened. It was broad daylight, and they pulled up in an alley. A man walked up to the car, and he looked like he was up to no good. He was tall, his hair was not cut, he had a rough beard, his eyes were red, and he had a mean look on his face.

He remember sitting in the back seat, wondering why was he at such a scary place. His father acted like it was no problem being in the alley, but his father never said anything to him. When the man walked up to the car, he and his father spoke for a bit; then the young man saw his father hand the man some money, and the man gave his father a couple of bags with what looked like grass in them. At the time, he did not know what it was, but he assumed it was not anything good.

Some people do not understand that the actions in which they engage in front of their young children can have an affect on the future of those children. The young man could have decided that was normal behavior and opted to follow in his father's footsteps and turn to drugs when he grew up. He decided when he was young that it was not a good idea to do drugs. He saw how the other people in that alley looked, and he did not want to end up like them. I also decided that drugs were no good. I had promised myself, to protect my younger brother for the rest of his life. I have tried to keep him from being in situations like the one the young man was in, that day with his father.

Some might wonder how I can call my father "absent", when in many ways, it seems as if he had been around. This is an example of how someone can be right in front of you, but you still do not have a relationship with that person or even really know who he is. I did not know my father. Since he was only around occasionally, I saw him as an empty shell, with no love or emotion inside.

I only saw my father when my mother sent me to visit him. I saw my father more when I was young, but that changed, as I got older. If a person is in your presence but does not interact with you or hardly notices you that person is still absent, in your heart and mind. As a little boy, I was never able to build that father and son bond, with my absent father.

# Chapter Four

# An Absent Father's Broken Promises

For years, my father called me to wish me a happy birthday a few days late. This is how I knew, and ultimately accepted, that my father did not love me enough to remember the day when his first-born son took his first breath. On a number of occasions, I felt my father was not genuine. He called occasionally and asked why I never called him. I just told him, "I don't know," but I realized it was because I just did not have anything to say to my absent father. I knew he only called after he got pressure from someone else to do it.

I have struggled with hate and trust issues throughout my life. My father often said, "Son, I will come watch you play football," but he didn't show up. I was so disappointed. I can only remember one game to which my father came, out of all the years I played. As a young boy with a father who played semi-pro football, I wanted to make him proud, even though I did not have a good relationship with him. My father did not even attend my wedding. His brothers came from hours away. He said his knee was injured. I was hurt that he did not come, but I hid it from others.

I guess a small piece of you never grows up. You still look for the approval of your parents and you continuously want to make them proud. You still love getting confirmation that you have accomplished something in line with what your parent had planned for you. It is good to feel loved by your parents. So many people enjoy going back home for the holidays and lying in the same bed in which they slept while growing up, cuddling up with their parents as they watched holiday movies. That sense of parent appreciation is key to most people's lives. Even as an adult, you hate to disappoint your parents. As an adult, your mother can still give you that look or change her tone of voice, and you know you had better correct whatever upset her. So even though my father did not fulfill promises he made to me, I still wanted to make him proud, or at least be viewed as making better decisions than he did.

I am now 35 years old and I still want to make my father proud. All I have ever wanted from him is a relationship. A number of my friends did not have their fathers around very often, either, while growing up. We were forced to grow up quickly and become the men, or sometimes even the women, of the house. Most people understand that when dealing with children, even if you did not formally promise something, it is still a promise if you said you would do it. Even if you did not give specifics, a child is going to hold you to what you said you would do.

I have a nephew whose father suddenly passed away a few years back. I think about my nephew constantly, because he is now forced to grow up with his main male influence gone forever. It made me thankful that my father is still living. My nephew was a pre-teen when his father died. His father will never get to meet his first girlfriend, see him graduate, teach him how to drive, take him hunting, show him how to shave, or even take him to campus his first day of college. I am sad for my nephew, my sister, and his father. His father was not perfect, but when I saw him interact with my nephew, you could tell he loved him and wanted the best for his son. I have made it my mission to see that he becomes a great young man and gets an education. I see so many of the qualities of his father in him.

We take for granted that our parents will be there tomorrow. The things we plan to share with our parents may never get shared. They may never get to hear our best ideas or dreams. We have to take today to make the best day with our parents.

Since my father broke so many promises, I want to make sure I fulfill promises I make to my children and other young people with whom I interact. A man's word should be golden and not broken. If I cannot do something

I said I would do, it is my responsibility to communicate that to my children and find a way to make it up to them.

One of the main reasons I want to be financially independent is because I want to be able to do anything I want with my children, when I want to do it. I want to take them to foreign countries to experience things I have only read about in books or seen on television. I pray daily that I will be the best father I can be to my children. When I die, I want to my children to know I gave my all to ensure they had everything they could ever need to be successful. As long as I am alive, I want to be a present father. I want to keep as many promises as possible. I never want to have to tell my children I cannot do something because I feel something else is more important.

My children and my nephews need me to be present in their lives. An absent father feels it is OK to break promises. I am lucky that my mother and my uncle fulfilled the promises my absent father did not. So many children who are relying on their mothers to keep the promises their absent fathers did not keep. A mother should not really have to keep her promises and the father's promises as well.

I saw my mother struggle. I am sure my father also broke promises to her. He had potential, when he was in college and possibly on his way to becoming a millionaire from playing in the National Football League. He did not live up to the promise to do everything he could to take care of his children. He is not unique; thousands of fathers are doing the same thing. But it is not acceptable to get a woman pregnant, and leave her to raise the child you conceived together. My heart breaks for the 15- and 16-year-old girls who are forced to raise their children without the fathers in the picture.

I heard of a young man who was 26 with 10 children here in Oklahoma. So in that situation, who is at fault? He is at fault, but not 100 Percent. He is an absent father in the worse way. He has no plans to be involved in the lives of his children. He has no plan to even make a promise to his children. I also heard a majority of the women knew he had a number of children, but they slept with him, anyway, and without using protection. This guy is a red flag; he will do whatever these women allow him to get away with. If a woman doesn't get to know a man before she sleeps with him, she is bound to repeat the mistakes of his previous women. Somewhere in this man's past, he was not shown the proper way to handle his life. He has an absent father.

Even if his father were around, he still might have

made the decisions he made. We all know people who had their mothers, fathers, and grandparents in their lives, but they still bring disgrace upon their families. I think if our young men and women have their fathers in their lives, they may start to make better choices. It is not a guarantee, but it cannot hurt.

The father is needed to teach his daughter that men should not lie to her, and they should treat her with respect. The absent father does not have the chance to do that. He has no input on how his daughter should handle situations when a boy disrespects her. He also does not have the opportunity to defend her or protect her when she needs him. She may have to grow up looking for that father figure in her life, and she may pick bad choices for partners, which could in turn start a cycle of abusive relationships. Her father also needs to teach her the importance of not relying on a man to take care of her. He must tell her she is worth the world, and she can own things without a man to purchase them for her. The father should stress the importance of ownership and achieving the highest level of education.

A father is needed to teach his son how to treat a young lady and how to be a man of the house. He needs to stress the importance of financial freedom and staying out of trouble. Young men of color are often the most vulnerable for being incarcerated. It is the father's responsibility to educate his son on the importance of making good choices and being a leader. He must advocate for his son so he'll be able to identify bad situations and use his mind to get out of those situations. For example, if his the knows his friends are up to no good, it is important for the son to understand he should stay away from them and not involve himself in this type of behavior.

I have been in multiple situations where I had to make the decision to either go along with what others were doing, or be a leader by doing what was right. I cannot say I always made the best decisions, but I think I heard my uncle and my mother in the back of my mind, telling me I knew what the best decision was – and their voices kept me from making some of the worse decisions.

My uncle always pushed me to be a leader. He knew I had leadership skills and he wanted me to showcase them. Our young boys and girls are our future leaders, and we must push them to realize their potential. Some of the best motivational speakers and business people were making poor decisions when they were young. They may have been thieves, liars or negative people, but they turned their lives around and took their leadership skills in a positive direction.

The same young man who is a leader in a gang could become the leader of a nonprofit organization. A young lady who leads a pack of mean girls in high school could be the leader of her own high-tech start-up. We must show our children there are alternatives to the lives their negative friends have chosen. Our children are our future, and it is our responsibility to provide the avenue for them to realize their potential.

If a child's father breaks promises, it can be heart-breaking. Our children have enough to worry about these days with the influence of drugs, cyber bullying, sex, and alcohol. They do not need to deal with broken promises from their fathers. I know mothers break promises as well, and they do not get a pass, but the single mothers are there every day, taking care of their children, while the absent fathers may show up every once in a while.

The single mothers are fulfilling their promises to their children every day. If my mother ever broke a promise, she did everything she could to explain why this happened, and she tried to make it up to us. I am not saying fathers can't break a few promises, but if they do, they should communicate to their children why they did so, and strive to compensate in some other way.

The last thought you want a child to have is that his/her father or mother breaks promises. This fosters feelings of disappointment. The child also loses trust in the parents. If we want our children to grow up and keep their promises to others, we must do the same. Our ancestors died for us. They fulfilled their promise to make a better life for us, so we have to do the same for our children. We can't make excuses. We are the adults, after all – not the children.

# Chapter Five

## Mother,

## Why Doesn't He Love Me?

As a young boy, I felt my absent father did not love me and that there may have been something wrong with me. I often sat and cried about why my father chose not to appreciate the young adult I was becoming. He fathered another little boy when I was in middle school and I began to distance myself further from my absent father. I cried to my mother, asking her, "Why doesn't he love me and take care of me like he does his new son?" I was under the impression that he was being present with his new son but he was not as active in his life either.

I knew it broke my mother's heart to see me that way, but she never said anything bad about my absent father. She loved my father with all her heart and wanted him to be a better person than he was. She always told my brother and me to pray for our father. Soon, the tears turned into a strong dislike of my father. I convinced myself I did not need him, and I put my energy toward making my mother, brother, and uncle proud at any cost.

Since I believed my absent father did not love me, I did not even want to hear his name or discuss him. People sometimes asked, "So how is your father?" and as years went by, my answer went from "Good" to "I don't care." It is sad that so many children have to share the same feelings as I did. How do we expect our children to love others when they believe their fathers do not love or appreciate them? Single or even married mothers all over the world have to explain or apologize for the father's actions or lack of presence.

My mother did not sign up to be a single mom. She did not plan to raise two boys on her own. She was in the same situations as so many other women: She chose a partner, but her partner did not live up to his side of the deal. He was able to go on living his life, apparently with little regard for my brother and me.

I was bullied in elementary school and ridiculed in middle school. But I never cried as much as when I began to believe my father did not love me or want to be in my life. I do not know if a piece of my soul yearned for my father's love, but I can remember growing up and wanting nothing more than to be loved by my father. I knew my mother loved me – that was a given – but I wanted the love of my father, too. I have spoken with other adults who had absent fathers, and they feel the same way. They also questioned why their fathers did not love them.

As children, we take situations to the extreme. As an adult, I now understand my father loved me, but he did not show me this when I was a child. During a conversation with a friend of mine, she said she wondered if there was something wrong with her and that was why her father was not around. So many young girls feel that same way. How do we expect them to find respectful men who cherish them when they did not know the love of their own fathers?

Girls who do not have fathers in their lives may fall into bad relationships. This is not to say a girl whose father is in her life cannot suffer the same fate, but we see the previous scenario far more often with girls who have absent fathers. I feel most girls with absent fathers still grow up to have meaningful relationships, as my friend does, but she has also allowed herself to be involved in unhealthy relationships with men who took advantage of her.

She still yearns for a relationship with her father, but she does not know how to start the process. I've advised her to approach her father and find a way to spend even 30 minutes with him, but it is difficult for her to muster up the courage to do it. Even as an adult, she is convinced he does not want to be part of her life or that he does not love her enough to try to be in her life or that of her children.

I remember sitting in the car with my mother and my younger brother and crying inconsolably when I was a young boy. Most people experience their first heartbreak from the opposite sex; my first heartbreak was from my father. He broke my heart by not being a present father. I am sure my father and other absent fathers may say they tried to be in the lives of their children, but they just didn't have the money to buy gifts, their work schedules made it difficult to come around, or even that the relationship with the mother made regular contact impossible. But I speak for so many young children when I say, "We do not care."

How do we expect a five-year-old boy or girl to understand any of those excuses? All we know is that we want our fathers around, but they are absent. I know my mother and father had arguments and fights like any other couple, but a young child can't relate that to the fact that the father is not around much.

It's not necessarily good to make excuses, but I firmly believe if a child does not experience love from his parents, it will affect him, as he becomes an adult. I do not remember saying "I love you" to my father until I became an adult. If I did say it, I must have said it because I felt an obligation to do so; I don't think there would have been any emotion behind it. My father must have said he loved me before I was an adult, but I do not remember it. Since I know the feeling of not being loved, I make sure I tell my children I love them as often as possible. I do not want them to feel the way I did.

All children deserve to feel loved. They are blessings and they cannot choose their parents. The anger I harbored against my father was directly related to my feeling that he did not love me. The tears I shed for him were wasted. In my mind, he did not care that I sat in my room, crying, because he was not around. I didn't want my uncles, friends, or grandparents; I wanted my father, and I wanted him to love me. Even as an adult, I sometimes struggle to find my identity and wonder if the ideas or projects I undertake will impress my father. I am now 35 years old, and I still look for that love from him.

I am glad he now expresses more emotions and love toward my siblings and me. There are too many men and women who are not experiencing this. They still are having difficulty forgiving their fathers and are still hurting from all the damage their absent fathers caused. They are clueless on how to start a conversation with their fathers or their children's fathers to see if a relationship can be built.

A child who does not have a father around should not use that as an excuse not to be successful. He should use that as a motivator to work as hard as possible to be the best person he can be. Too many times, we allow ourselves to be labeled or marginalized. I refused to do that. I wanted to be the best at anything I did. This drive and passion was in me from a young age. I just had to have someone bring it out of me.

That person was my middle school coach, a fiery man named Scotty. I started playing football in the 7th grade. I was small and quick, so naturally, he tried me out at running back. He saw I had talent, so he allowed me to become his starting running back. I was so proud, because I was playing the same position my father played, and I just knew he would be proud of me. Unfortunately, I do not recall his coming to any game but one my whole time in middle school. Instead of allowing that to frustrate me, I decided to use my anger as motivation to become a good football player. Coach Scotty wanted to try me out on defense as well, because he knew I was a good athlete. When he moved me to defense, I had the second-most tackles on the team my 8th-grade year. Once again, these were moments my father missed.

I did not start playing football because I thought he

would be proud; I started playing because I generally enjoyed playing. Even though Coach Scotty believed in me and was serving as a father figure, he still discouraged me. I believe this is one of the first times I remember being told I could not do something or achieve something. Coach Scotty told me I was a good athlete, but that I was too small to play high school football. Now here was a man, saying this to an 8th-grade boy.

He tried to crush my dream, but I did not allow him to do that. I used his lack of support to push me to play football in high school. Not only did I play high school football, but also I beat out a few kids who were larger and more gifted at running back than I was. How did I do it? First of all, I was a good kid and I tried to stay out of trouble. The other guys often got in trouble for being late to practice, so I got to start one game. After that, I never sat on the bench again. I played on offense and defense and I was 3rd in the state in kickoff returns.

I always remembered Coach Scotty's negative words. They hurt a bit at the time, but in hindsight, I wonder if that was his way of pushing me to see what I was made of. I finished my high school career and went on to college to play my freshman year. I had made it as a college football player when my coach told me it would never happen. We must encourage our children to shoot for the moon, because at least they will land in the clouds.

I wondered if my father's oldest son playing football did not bring him closer to me, then what would? I continued to feel my father did not love me while I attended middle school. I probably reasoned that since I was playing football, my father would eventually come around and coach me after practices or games. I assumed he would want to share all his practice techniques with me, but that did not happen. I suspect one reason was because my father did not know how to have a conversation with me. He did not know me. He was around from time to time, and we sometimes visited him when I was younger, but he did not know much about who I was or who I wanted to be.

I never remember lying on my father's shoulder when I was sick or down about something. I never remember my father reading a book to me. My father is a college graduate, and I never remember him helping me with my homework or making me study even when I did not have homework. His job was to push and lead me to greatness, but he chose not to do that. He instead elected to wait and see what type of person I would become.

He is proud of me now, but where was he when I was struggling to understand what I read in 2nd grade? Where was he when I got beat up by a neighborhood bully? Where was my father when I had to study eight hours some days in college just so I can comprehend the computer programming code on which I was going to be tested that week? My father was not there.

I had to send my mother money when I was in school. I gave my mother and brother cars because they needed them. I had to be the man of the house, and I could barely put my own shoes on the correct feet. Where was my father? He was absent.

My mother did not deserve to have to struggle the way she did. She did not deserve to worry about which bill she would not pay so her boys could eat. She deserved the best things this world could provide. I want to give her that. I know my mother and almost every other mother would say she had the best thing the world could offer when she had my brother and me. She is married now to a loving husband, but I still want to take care of my mother before I die.

"Mother, why does my father not love me?" That question is being asked of single mothers all over the world. Mothers have had to answer that question for hundreds of years. That same question transcends race, socio-economic status, religion, and sexual orientation. I remember seeing the disappointment on my mother's face when I asked her that question. All she could say is that my father loved me and we should continue to pray for him. My mother will tell you she is not a saint, but that response, to me, was saintly. Mothers have to field difficult questions daily, and they have to just bite their tongues and speak positively about their child's absent father. Even if they don't want to say anything positive about the father, many mothers are taking the high road and just asking for prayers for their children's fathers.

# Chapter Six

## Growing Up With Hate for Another Person

I grew up hating the fact that my father was not around and that he left my mother to take care of two young boys with minimal assistance. As a teenager, I decided the hate I felt for my father was like being in prison. I could not move on or get over the things my father had done. I struggled with the reality of growing up with an absent father my entire young life. I knew it was a sin in the Bible to hate my father, and I wanted to go to heaven, so one day, at age 15, I decided not to say that I hated my absent father. I told myself that I forgave him for all the things he had done to my family. At the time I wrote this story, I looked back and wondered if I just said I would not hate my father because I knew it was the right thing to say.

I remember one day speaking to my father on the phone, and he asked, "Why don't you call me?" I replied angrily, "We never know where you are; you always have a different number, and you barely call us." He was so upset with me for telling him the truth that he said, "Oh, OK," and hung up on me. After that, I told myself I did not care if I ever spoke to him or saw him as long as I lived. I also recall my father's saying he was getting married, but he never asked me or anyone from my family to attend. I was hurt but relieved, because I felt no one could get mad at me when I did not invite him to my own wedding. I decided to be the bigger man, though, and I invited him to my wedding – but he did not come.

I wonder how many people in this world harbor similar hate or dislike for their absent fathers. When I was younger, I allowed my hate to control my life. It was not healthy. I did not like to open up to people about anything because I did not trust that they were genuine. In the past, when I was in the same room as my father, I tried to do everything I could not to make eye contact or speak with him. A sense of rage had built up inside of me. To a certain extent, it was good to have this anger, because it helped keep me focus on how I wanted to treat people when I grew up.

I loved everything about my father's side of the family except for my father. It pained me to have hate in my heart for him, and I often sat and cried because I did not know what to do or how I should feel. My mother tried to under- stand my internal turmoil, but I really never opened up to her about my true feelings for my father.

My father's family knew he did not do right by us, and they were not to happy with him, either. Thinking back, I realize my anger could have boiled over into an argument with my father. I do not think I would have ever hit him, but I was always afraid of what might happen if he and I ever got into an altercation. When you are so hurt, you feel you have nothing to lose, and you can make irrational mistakes.

An example of how hate for another person can be dangerous involves my cousin and my uncle. My uncle made promises to his two girls and his son, but would fail to keep them. He was present, but he put other things ahead of his children. This is a problem, because his children grew up expecting their father to constantly lie to them. They loved their father, but they could not trust that he loved them enough to make time for them over other activities, such as hanging out with his friends.

As a father, it is important to make personal time with your children. Just being in the same room is not enough. It is also difficult, when you have broken so many promises, to effectively build a relationship. My uncle wanted to be a great father to his children, but he allowed external forces to keep his attention versus his children from time to time.

I spent a great deal of time with my cousin when we were younger. He was the same age as my brother and he came over on weekends to spend the night with us, since he had sisters. I loved him as if he was my brother. All three of us formed a brotherly bond. As he became an adult, he dealt with some of the same issues I did. His father was married to my cousin's mother, but they fought often. That caused a strain on the children. Sometimes when I was at their house, an argument would erupt and my cousins would start crying.

Today, I think about how important it is to make sure that if my wife and I have a disagreement, our children are not around to witness it, or that we handle it in a respectful manner. My cousin started to develop a strong dislike for my uncle. Initially he cherished his father, but he wasn't as close to his father as he wanted to be. Much like my father, my uncle is a very charismatic person. He has the talent to speak to anyone and makes friends easily. Unfortunately, he has neglected his children in certain situations.

It was difficult for my cousin while growing up, because he did not get to do the father-son things that I missed as well, like fishing, hunting, and working on projects around the house. His father was there, but they did not build a relationship, which makes him an absent father, because again, you can still be an absent father even if you are in the same room as your child. It is sad how some fathers or mothers feel spending time with their children is watching television in the same room. If parents do not engage with their children, they might as well not even be in the room.

As my cousin grew older and started his own family, he decided he would do everything he could to be in the lives of his children and their mother. He wanted his father to have a better relationship with his grandchildren than he did when he was growing up. My cousin was disappointed that his father did not initially reach out very much to get to know his grandchildren. It bothered him to the extent that he built a hatred for my uncle. My uncle's girlfriend had a granddaughter with whom my uncle spent more time than his own, which infuriated my cousin.

I recall a conversation we had about our absent fathers. We both shared how emotional it is for a child who wants to have a better relationship with his father, but it does not happen. Of course, we both looked at ourselves to see if there was something wrong with us that prevented our absent fathers from being present fathers. I revealed to him that I had unhealthy hatred for my father when I was younger and until adulthood. I explained that when you carry hate for a person, that person is winning.

Sometimes I wondered if they both were just oblivious to their absence. My cousin was upset and I was concerned over whether his relationship with his father would be irreversible. For my part, I had already begun the forgiving process. I let my cousin know I use to have some hard feeling toward my father, but I let them go so I could move forward. Sometimes, it's good to have a friend to pull you away from the ledge.

I am so proud that as of today, my uncle is active in the lives of his children and his grandchildren. He and my cousin have a better relationship. They even went camping this past summer, and the kids loved it. This shows the power a father can have when he steps up and takes care of his children. If this relationship had not been mended, my uncle may have missed years of joy with his children and grandchildren.

He may have grown old without the love of the children whom he helped bring into this world. My uncle is happy and my cousin is happy. They will still have issues now and then, but their relationship is strong now. My father is human and he has made mistakes, as I have myself. I really feel he is sorry for many of the things he has done in his life. The last time I went out to eat with him, I could tell he really enjoyed the opportunity to sit down and talk with me. That meant a lot to me. I no longer nurse a hatred for my father. In my view, he has grown to appreciate life and the relationships he can have for the rest of his life.

My father will not be here forever, and I regret that we missed so many years, but I am free to communicate with him now, and I know he will welcome my communication and respond to me. Our father-son relationship is what it should be now. The men in my family are very proud men, and it is hard for them to admit when they are wrong, but I have seen so much growth of the men in my family. They are appreciating the time they spend with their children even more, because they realize time is short. They may not know this, but they have inspired me to take full advantage of life and try to do everything possible to stay in my children's life.

Hate is such a powerful emotion, and it controls so many of us on a daily basis. Hating my father akin to hating myself. I looked down on myself because I felt my father did not love me. I had to push that thought out of my mind. Writing down my thoughts has been therapeutic, and it has allowed the ball and chain that I was carrying to be released. A man once said that letting a person get to you is like letting him live in your head rent-free. My father no longer deserved to live rent-free in my head, but he did deserve to live rent-free in my heart.

My thoughts and prayers go out to all the children of absent fathers who have hate or dislike in their hearts for their fathers. I know how hard it is to let things go, because I am a stubborn person. In deciding to forgive, I chose happiness and peace over hate. To say that a weight has been lifted, is an understatement. Freedom is worth everything it takes to achieve it.

# Chapter Seven

## The Influence of a Strong Single Mother

My mother, brother, and I moved back to Tulsa when he was four years old. My mom lived the single mothers' life, making sure her boys got up and went to school, had a place to sleep, had food, and grew up with some discipline. Things were difficult for us, but we had one another. My mother worked as a cosmetologist about 12-16 hours a day. She's a strong, funny, and independent woman, and some of my personality came from growing up with her.

My mother worked various jobs to take care of her two boys. I always saw her working, and that strongly influenced me as I grew up. Having two children and being a single mother can be challenging, but my mother did not worry about that. She was not the type of person to blame her situation on others. She took responsibility for her actions and tried to make a better life for us to improve our odds of being successful.

My relationship with my mother was very strong while I was growing up. She loved us with all her heart and we were her world, but like any single mom, she faced many problems. Bills had to be paid, which meant she had to work long hours. Most days, my brother and I stayed by ourselves when we came home from school.

We were "latch-key kids," and there are millions like us in the world. That means we come home from school to an empty house, because our parents are elsewhere. I knew my mother loved me and had to work long hours so my brother and I could live normal young lives. My mother spent as much time as possible with us. Even after she got off work late, she liked to ask us about our day and how our lives were going.

I learned the value of working to take care of a family, no matter the cost, from my mother. I knew we all had to come together to make everything work. I learned I might have to initially sacrifice time with my family to take care of them, and that was a sacrifice I had to make. I also learned not to use work as an excuse for not spending time with my wife or children. Like any other mother, my mother wanted the best for her children. She wanted us to grow up to respect and appreciate everything we have.

I quickly found out I did not want to work all those hours to make a living, so I was fortunate that she pushed education in our household. My mother was one of the smartest people I knew growing up. She had an ability to identify with people and speak to them on their level. People felt comfortable around her and shared their deepest secrets with her.

Respect was a must for my younger brother and me. My mother insisted that we say “yes, ma’am,” “no, ma’am, “yes, sir,” “no, sir,” “thank you,” “please” and “excuse me.” She also required us to call her “mother” instead of “mom” or “momma.” This taught me the importance of respecting others, especially my elders. The discipline my mother in-stilled in her house, helped shape the way I act as an adult.

I also learned the value of interacting with others from my mother. When my brother and I went to the beauty shop where our mother worked, we observed the unique interactions of the beauticians and their customers. They talked about everything: relationships, politics, current events, men, and the most current gossip. I was always an observant young boy and loved interacting with my mother’s clients.

I had to interact, anyway, because my mother always told them everything that happened in my life, good or bad. I didn’t mind that so much as a young boy, but as I became a young adult, it started to embarrass me. I would walk into the shop and the ladies would giggle and bring up something my mother had just told them about me. Even as an adult, when I walk into my mother’s shop, I wait for one of her customers to ask me about something going on in my life, but I eventually got used to it, and I knew they felt as if they had known me for years and they care about me.

My sister has been raising her children as a single parent, with limited support from her children's fathers. She does not get the chance to be absent. She is present every day to ensure that her children know she loves them and that she will do anything possible to help them be successful. I have seen my sister work two jobs to support her family. I have watched her give her time to other young people. She is always tired, but she has made a promise to herself to do what she can to influence young people to be their best. That is powerful. It takes a special person to teach children who are not their own to improve themselves and strive for success.

My sister does not get paid to volunteer her time to help motivate the youth at schools, nor does she get paid to raise her own children. Her very existence revolves around improving the lives of others. In fact, she tracked me down when I was 15. She and I share the same father, but we have different mothers. She knew my mother's first name but not her last name. She looked in phone book under my mother's first name and our father's last name, but she found my name instead, and decided to call.

She wanted to know her other siblings from her father's side of the family.

When I spoke with her, I did not know what to think at first. I had heard I had siblings on my father's side of the family, but I had never met or spoken with them. Once I met her, our relationship grew stronger and stronger. I found out I had nephews and I was excited to meet them.

My sister did not grow up with me, but once she connected with my brother and me, she did everything she could to continue building a relationship with us. She has been one of the most supportive people of any of my projects or ideas. She helps push me to be better. She has taken on the responsibility of a single parent like a champ, and has ensured that her children have had great Christmases since they were born. The fathers may not have been as supportive or present as she would have liked, but she did not use that as an excuse for her children not to be in the best clothes possible. She did not use it as an excuse for her children not to go to an excellent school. My sister is making sure the single mother label is not a hindrance, but rather an opportunity to achieve greatness.

Being a single mother does not have to be a negative label. Single mothers are embracing change and are striving for excellence. There are still mothers who are down and out because of their circumstances, but there is hope ahead. We have to reach out to them and let them know we love and support them. Our strong single mothers are entrepreneurs, community leaders, educators, politicians, and more. We must ensure all women and men see that single mothers are a driving force in our communities.

My single mother raised my brother and me while being an entrepreneur. For most of her life, she did not get a paycheck; she only received payment for services rendered. When she provided the best hair service as possible, people gave her money for it. Our single mothers are educating our youth in the schools, in our churches, and as heads of the households.

Our men are traditionally supposed to be the leading forces in our communities and households, but with the epidemic of absent fathers, the single mothers have had to fill the voids. Dr. Martin Luther King Jr. had a dream, and I also have a dream. My dream is that our single mothers and absent fathers will open the lines of communication with each other and work on a plan so they may both have input into the lives of their children. I have a dream that our little boys and little girls will have the support of their fathers or father figures. I have dream that our absent fathers will take the steps to build relationships with their children.

My dream is an achievable one that must start with you. You may not be a single mother; you may not be an absent father, either, but you know someone who is. Share this book with those people. Share your thoughts about how you can help them build better relationships with their previous partners for the good of their children. I have a dream that our villages will continue to support our youth, our single mothers, our single fathers, and our single grandparents who are all raising the future leaders – or future prison inmates.

There are over one million black men in American prisons and jails today. Most of them did not have fathers while growing up, and they made decisions a father may have been able to curtail. A percentage of them did not have mothers in their lives. We have to put our arms around the youth of today and let them know they are loved. If we do not do it, a pimp, a gang member, a pedophile, or a jail cell will become the mothers and fathers of some of our youth.

# Chapter Eight

## Breaking the Curse of The Absent Father

As a young boy, I witnessed many things, such as people who were not faithful to their significant others. I told myself I would at least do everything I could to be in the lives of my children. I was fortunate that I did not have children until later in life. I did not get married until I was 29, and I did not have my first child until I was 31. But even if I had a child before I was married, I believe I would have been a big part of my child's life. I wanted to complete my education and start a career before I started a family, and I was able to finish high school and earn my undergraduate and graduate degrees. At the very least, I can tell my children their father is educated, so they will hopefully live up to the standards I've set for them.

I decided as a young man that I would break the cycle of being an absent father. No matter what my situation was, I was going to fight to be in the lives of my children. I did not want to just take care of them financially; I wanted to be part of their daily lives. To break this curse of my father not regularly being in my life, I pledged to first establish myself so no one could ever say I was not fit to take care of my children or be an integral part of their lives.

I wanted to ensure that I had my education, my own

car, my own place to live, and my own money. I did not want to have to ask anyone for anything. I forced myself to be independent, and even when I was struggling; I found a way to pay my bills. When I first got out of college, I worked a commission-only job. It was very difficult to make money because I was trying to build a territory that had already been picked over. I routinely brought in $500 for the entire month.

For my first three years out of college, I never made over $30,000, but by being frugal, I was still able to save enough money to finance my first house for $82,500. To break the curse, you have to refuse to be cursed. I could have found myself in some negative situations with past relationships, but even so, if I had conceived a child with one of the women I dated, that child would have been a member of the Carolina family and would have been loved and taken care of for life. That was my thought process. This may all sound simplistic, but it is in fact difficult, because I have not always been in the right mindset as a young adult. I was a bit wild, and even though I knew I didn't want have children at that time, I didn't always make the best decisions to prevent that from happening.

Since I was blessed with my father's charm, I loved to

be around as many wonderful women as possible. Some women are attracted to a guy with his own stuff, and I wanted people to know I could take care of myself and I was responsible. As a younger man, I figured if a girl got pregnant, we could just have an abortion, and that would be that. But later, I realized I had to make better decisions and truly grow up. I started to consider whether I would be comfortable having a baby with the person I was with at the time. That is a difficult discussion to have with a virile, confident young man, but it was necessary.

That curse of the absent father is real, but it's not an excuse to abandon responsibilities. I have heard stories about people making excuses as to why their sons became absent fathers. The rationale has ranged from saying he wasn't ready to be a father, to assertions that he is too young to take care of a baby, or that the girl is mistreating him and he doesn't want to be with her any longer.

Parents must stop making excuses for their children. Children must be taught there are consequences for their actions. Parents must understand that otherwise, a single mother will be raising their grandchild. While single mothers are out there struggling to make it day to day, absent fathers are taking pictures of their money and posting them on social media.

A real man takes his money and uses it to make sure his children are fed even before he himself is fed. I find it annoying that so many great fathers in the world do not get enough credit for all the things they do, because the absent fathers overshadow them. But ultimately, present fathers will get the respect they deserve.

I see young men on a daily basis and I wonder how their lives will end up when they are adults. I wonder if their fathers are in their lives, or if they have absent fathers. We need strong, educated, and caring young men in our communities. These young men will one-day father children, so if we raise them right they will hopefully transfer that knowledge to their children. Responsible young men will also mentor other young men and that is one way to break the curse. Education is key to helping our communities excel. Present fathers must give back and mentor young men in our communities so they will know how to be a present father and not an absent father.

According to a Huffington Post article from 2013, 4.1 million single mothers are living in poverty in the United States. It is difficult enough to take care of yourself when you are entrenched in poverty; just imagine taking care of one or two children under those conditions. How do we expect our young people to break the cycle of poverty if they are surrounded by it?

An article from the New York Times points out a North-South divide for households with single mothers raising children. The northern states have a lower percentage of single mothers raising children alone than do the southern states. The absence of a father in the household continues to increase inequality and poverty in the world. How do we expect mothers to raise their children while they are working minimum wage or low-paying jobs?

How do we expect those young children to get the same educational opportunities as those who do not live in poverty? It does not happen often. If we can increase our girls' education levels, we will increase their opportunity for better jobs, and hopefully decrease their interest in becoming mothers before age 21. And even if they do end up becoming single mothers, the better education will prepare them to face the challenge they may encounter.

We also must push entrepreneurship and innovation to young girls so they can once again live up to their potential rather than focusing on what boys think they should look like or act like. Women are powerful, and we must harness that power and focus it on the most productive activities that will help enrich their lives.

Teen pregnancy is decreasing in America, which is directly related to the young ladies seeing their mothers and grandmothers struggle to lead households with absent fathers. Women are also waiting later to have children. The national average is now 26 years of age. That is important, because as people age, their education level should proportionately increase along with their income level. Women are graduating college at a higher percentage than men, and they are purchasing homes at a higher percentage as well.

Well-prepared women aren't the only key to decreasing absent fathers, but if we teach our women the importance of delaying child-bearing until they have established themselves and set their goals, they will have better lives and should have the resources needed to raise families. The government should not have to be the financial fathers of our country, as they have been for years.

We break that cycle of the absent father through education of young boy and girls. Women must also be encouraged to make better choices on the men with whom they choose to have sexual relations, and they should be instructed to use birth control. We must teach our men that if they have sex with women, they must protect themselves and their partners by using condoms.

# Chapter Nine

## The Male Father Figure Who Changed My Life

Having a male role model for a young boy is very important. Too many times, a boy is forced to grow up in a single-mother household. Without strong mothers, this world would be worse off, because many young men would not have any guidance at all. I also recognize the single fathers and our stepfathers who are doing great work to help raise our future leaders.

My Uncle Sylvester (my father's brother) was a key figure who molded me into the man I eventually became. My uncle is a war veteran who worked most of his adult life for one company. He knew the meaning of hard work, sacrifice, and treating others with love and respect. He has been a deacon at his church for years and has spent countless hours mentoring young people. He is a role model in Moffett, Oklahoma. To me, he is the epitome of a present father, even though he is not my biological father and he doesn't have children of his own. He was there for my brother and me if we needed anything while we were growing up -- and even now.

From my first interaction with Uncle Sylvester, there was an instant connection. Probably since he never had children, he took to my brother and me from day one. He knew his brother was not doing right by his sons, or my mother. He considered it his duty to ensure that we had everything we needed, because we were part of his family. One Christmas, my mother was having a hard time paying the bills and was working so hard to make the holiday special for us, but she was coming up short. My uncle drove over an hour, took us to Toys R- Us, and bought our Christmas gifts. My mother couldn't help but cry after seeing her two boys so happy.

Uncle Sylvester taught my brother and me how to be men and take care of business at all times. He always told me, "No matter what, take care of your business." My uncle was a great role model for us on how a man should take care of a family. In his mind, we were almost like his own children. I remember looking into my uncle's eyes and seeing unconditional love for my brother and me. He did not take care of us because he was going to win any awards or special accolades; he did it because he felt it was the right thing to do.

My uncle was always active in the church and used biblical principles when talking with my brother and me. He knew I had a deep resentment for my father, but he always told me, "No matter what, he is your father, and you need to respect him." My relationship with my uncle grew even closer as I became older. Whenever I had a problem, I called him to get advice. My relationship with my uncle bothered my father; he felt my uncle had overstepped his bounds and was trying to make him look bad. When I heard how my father had a problem with my uncle, I got upset, because in my mind, my uncle should not have had to step up; my father should have been there from day one.

As the years passed, I did not even think to call my father on Father's Day. I instead called my uncle to wish him a happy Father's Day. He tried to make it to our football games and special events. That meant a great deal to me, because I had become accustomed to my father's making promises and letting me down every time. I did not spend much time with my uncle, because he lived almost two hours away, but he made sure we did not go very long without seeing him. I remember feeling so bad for my uncle because I suspected he was helping my mother with my brother and me out of obligation, but as I looked back at the situation with the eyes of an adult, I realize he loved us with all his heart and wanted the best for us.

I recall countless times when my uncle helped me get through tough moments in my life. When I was in college, I took difficult computer programming classes and had to memorize lines of code. It was horrible, because I already had a learning disability that made it difficult for me to remember what I read. I had to spend eight hours on some days, just studying code. I frequently called my uncle for encouragement, and he repeatedly reminded me why I was attending college: It was to get a degree and become a productive adult. He told me that while I might find the classes difficult at the moment, once I got my grade at the end of the semester, it would all be worthwhile.

My uncle never let me use my limitations as an excuse, and that is what a loving father does. He did not tolerate mediocrity, and he always pushed me to be a better student. My uncle used to tell me I needed to make my money with a pen, rather than with my back, which was excellent advice. He worked in a paper plant for over 35 years, and most of his years working there involved hard labor. He is just one example of all the exceptional men out there helping raise children who are not their own. He also wanted to make sure I was strong and that I kept my family first. One of the most important comments my uncle ever made was that people are put on this earth to disappoint others, but the ones who will disappoint the most are family members.

My uncle was the first man to whom I felt

comfortable saying, "I love you" when we spoke to or saw each other. I had great relationships with my other uncles, too, and I knew they loved me, because they took care of me and made sure I felt loved. But I did not have the father-son love like I did with my Uncle Sylvester. Now, when we end every phone conversation or when we are parting ways after a visit, we say, "I love you" to each other. That means so much to me. Those three words showed me I can love my son and say "I love you" as much as I want, no matter who hears. I hung and kiss my son because my uncle showed me how to love. He taught me there is nothing wrong with showing your love for another male family member.

I often think about all the people my uncle has helped. I have seen him countless times pay for family members to stay in hotels if they did not have enough money for the rooms themselves. He has dedicated his life to his church and its youth. He is a member of the local school board, and before he retired, he was a leader in the union for his company. He is a man who demands respect and gives respect where it is due. I can only hope to become half the man he is when I am finished on this Earth. I am proud to call him family. It doesn't matter if you are a guest or a lifelong friend; my Uncle Sylvester will treat you with dignity and open his doors to you.

My uncle has one peculiar trait: He tends to invade your space when he talks to you, and I guess he got that from being in the military. I always had to warn my girlfriends before I took them to Moffett to meet him so they would not get startled when he got very close to their faces to talk to them. Sometimes when he is speaking to someone, he looks like a mafia godfather, giving out orders. If you have a problem with personal space, my uncle will solve it for you. Your inner circle is his circle.

My uncle did not have to step in and help my mother with my brother and me, but he did so with joy and excitement. I hope I'll be able to show the love to my nephews that my uncle showed my brother and me. It is my job to everything I can to support her and my nephews as my uncle did my brother and me. He may not know it, but he taught me how I should be involved in other young men's lives. Our boys and young men need to know that men care for them and that someone other than their mothers care about their futures.

Uncle Sylvester never yelled at me or had to discipline me. He earned my respect from day one. I never wanted to disappoint him; all I wanted to do was make him proud. I know he is proud that I am writing this book as a way to deal with issues that have plagued me for over 30 years.

# Chapter Ten

## Lucky Me

I was luckier than most. Even though my father was absent most of the time, I had an exceptional support system. I have a great family on both my mother's side and my father's side. I have a strong, loving, independent mother, and I had a couple of grandfathers, a couple of grandmothers, and I have a number of uncles and aunts who have all loved and supported me my entire life. So many children do not have this support system, and they need it to help them develop into productive adults. I took away the positive traits from everyone in my life. I wanted to grow up and make my mother and uncle proud and be a good example for my younger brother. To this day, that is what drives me in my life.

I never like to make excuses but just think about how difficult it is for a child whose mother is on drugs, whose dad is not in the picture, whose uncle is in jail, and whose grandfather is in jail, and the child lives in low-income housing. How do we expect that child to escape this cycle? Perhaps no one in his or her immediate family has an education beyond high school. How is this child supposed to understand the importance of going to college? This is the reality for so many children around the world. How do we save them?

If my situation had been a bit different and I did not have the support system that I do, there is no telling how my life would have ended up. The saying that it takes a village to raise a child is so correct. My mother relied on multiple family members to help her raise my brother and me. Support systems are imperative to ensuring children grow up to be productive and successful adults.

Let's take Bobby, for example; he is a 7-year-old boy living in a single-mother home. His father is alive, but Bobby has never met him. Bobby's parents conceived him at age 16 while in high school. Bobby's parents broke up because his father did not think was ready to be a father.

Women can see how easy it is for a boy or man to walk away from responsibilities. The mothers generally do not walk away, although some do. Bobby's father continued to attend high school, but Bobby's mother had to drop out because she could not keep up with the work, and she had a few complications with the pregnancy. Bobby has watched his mother live on public assistance and move from house to house constantly. Bobby's grandmother is only 38 years old, which means she had his mother at age 15.

The cycle of having babies at a young age can go on for generations. Bobby's grandmother and his mother have had a difficult relationship, but she has always been there for him. His great-grandmother's mother is also still living, and she is 55- years old, which means she had his grandmother at age 16. There are no grandfathers in the picture.

Bobby's mother works a minimum-wage job and is barely making it. This has been the same cycle for three generations in his family. So who is at fault for this perpetual situation? No one, really but it has taken until the third generation for the words from previous generations to sink into reality.

Everyone has known a family in this same situation. Do you think Bobby's great-grandmother didn't tell her daughter she wanted her to make different decisions than she did, and so on down the line? It sometimes takes a few generations for the cycle to stop or at least improve. Bobby's mother constantly tells him he is, "The One." He has to make it out of the cycle and break the chain of previous generations. She focuses on trying to sit down and help him with his homework. She does not want her son to father a child at an early age, so she tells him his focus must be education.

She tells him girls will be there later in life, but they do not want an uneducated man. She explains to him there was no other male in the family who had graduated from college, and he must be the one to change that. She further advises that college is his way out of poverty, but she can't afford to send him, so if he wants a better life for himself and his mother, he must make something of himself.

With all the conversations she has with her son over the years, Bobby's mother eventually starts to believe her words for her own life. She looks at herself and decides she can't expect her son to heed her words; he needs to follow her actions. She makes a promise to her son that she will get her GED and they will do their homework together each night. Bobby's mother is finally able to achieve her goal of getting her GED, and she decides not to stop there: She earns a health care technical certification. Bobby sees how dedicated his mother is to making a better life for both of them. He continues to work hard in school and earns a scholarship to college.

Stories like this one are unfolding all over the world. It takes strong mothers and villages to break the cycle and helping young mothers raise their children to be productive adults. We have to save our children. The future leaders of our world could currently be living in poverty. Shouldn't children born to poor families have the right to be successful? Their minds and ideas can help change the world for the better. I have seen the power of education and of a family who loves and supports me.

We need to support our children with innovative programs. Imagine all the children who have never been on the wealthier side of town. Imagine all the children who have never visited a college campus. We must show our children the finer things in life so they will see hope instead of the jail cell or endless poverty.

Poverty is a generational issue. Many families are chronically poor; they have been poor and uneducated for generations. Now is the opportunity to break that cycle. This is the new generation, where hope is more than just a word. Families can lift themselves out of poverty, but it starts with education. My mother pushed our education because she knew it was our key out of poverty. She has never been a rich woman, but she was rich in her passion for her children. She frequently told my brother and me that we may not be rich, but we have our health and the lord. That stuck with me, because that message should be told to millions of struggling families.

There are more resources for children these days, but many young people are not taking advantage of their opportunities. One reason is they do not know about the opportunities, but also, they may not be seeking them. We have to want our children to be better than we are. A young single mother who is struggling to raise her child should be encouraged to know that women have made it through the same situation. They should find mentors who can help them achieve their goals, and never allow self-doubt to keep them from doing what they want to do in life.

I know a woman who got pregnant at 14 and again at 16. Most people would assume she'd be on assistance for the rest of her life. People may think her children would grow up to see their mother work minimum-wage jobs for the rest of her life. I was encouraged to hear her story. She got married when she was 17 to her children's father, but she decided to leave her husband because she suspected he just wanted her to keep having babies. He did not value her enough to want her to get an education. He wanted to keep her dependent on him without a way to support herself. She said it was difficult to make that decision, but it was one she had to make for the good of her children and herself.

How many times do you hear of a woman who is in a relationship with a man for 10-15 years? The woman is not the breadwinner; she stays at home with the children or works, but does not have a higher level of education. She is loyal to her boyfriend or husband, and then, he breaks up with her, and she is required to start over and try to support her children.

She does not have the education to secure a job that will net her the same money she is used to, so she has to downgrade her standard of living. The boyfriend or husband becomes an absent father and provides minimal child support payments. But even though she may be down, she does not have to be out.

Women are fighters, and that same woman can pull herself up and start taking small steps to regain control of her life. It starts with her focusing on bettering herself for the sake of her children. Education or entrepreneurship is the key to improving her situation.

That young lady who had two children by the time she was 16 ultimately made something of herself. She was able to get her GED, but she did not want to stop there. She decided to reach her goal of taking care of her children, she had to attain the highest level of education possible, so she earned her bachelor's and master's degrees. She did not allow her circumstances to keep her down. She was not going to be defined by being a 14-year-old mother. Her life has improved dramatically. She is now married with a huge house. She has grandchildren whom she is able to help raise and support.

The main accomplishment she enjoys is knowing that her children saw their mother earn her education and everything that she achieved as a result. Adversity can be an element of success. All successful people had to go through trying times. They may not have been raised in the same neighborhoods, but something has happened to them or their families, and they've refused to be defined by their adversity. Find your voice and speak it.

I always say I was lucky growing up because my mother decided I would be successful, even if it meant her giving up her life for it to happen. You cannot buy love like that. To lay down your life so someone else can succeed is the true meaning of love and sacrifice. My mother altered her life so her children could attend good schools and live in good neighborhoods. Millions of children are not that fortunate, but I firmly believe the lord is watching over them and their situations will improve. But that can only happen if we focus on our absent fathers and our single mothers.

Those two groups are the keys to prosperity of our world. If we can get more fathers to at least start building better relationships with their children, we will see a generation of flourishing young people. If we can focus on supporting single mothers and encouraging them to set and achieve goals, we will see even more single mother entrepreneurs, community leaders, educators, and politicians, which is needed in every country around the globe.

I want to reach that young boy or girl who thinks his or her life will be defined by being in government assistance programs. I want to reach that adult who feels their life is stuck in the current state. I want to reach that grandparent who feels he does not have an answer for how to support his family. My experience shows me that lives can be changed and enriched with hope, passion, a work ethic, and a big heart. You have to make the decision that you will not be a victim, but a victor, and you will see victory in your life. You will have setbacks, but that is part of life. What matters is how you handle your setbacks. I choose to handle them with a smile. Getting down in the dumps has never helped me achieve my goals.

Writing this book was a goal I put on the back burner for eight years while I pursued other avenues in my life, but I am glad I did that, because my experiences over the past eight years have allowed me to finish this book. A friend asked me a few months ago about this book and said, "Are you going to ever finish it?" He believed I had a good message and people needed to hear it. He motivated me to use my pain to reach my goal.

I have poured my life into this book, and I know others would like to write a book or achieve a goal. The way to do it is just to start. I think about all the young authors who are in poor neighborhoods. I think about all the small businesses that could be created if young people were educated on the importance of entrepreneurship.

If they want to be successful, they must do things that other successful people do. They have to spend hours working on a craft. I frequently use the facilities of the university from which I graduated as a base of operations where I can work on my ideas or products. Those who do not have college or university nearby can identify places in their homes that can be used as productive space, where they can write down ideas or plans.

# Chapter Eleven

## Saying Sorry and Asking for Forgiveness

As a 27-year-old man when I started writing this book, I looked back at my life and reflected on how angry I was about having an absent father. I had built up such a strong dislike for my father that if he had died, I do not think I would have shed one tear, or if I did, I would be crying because I was resentful that he had not been around enough. I always felt as if I was in a prison when I was dealing with my father. I knew in my heart I would be a great father and husband to my wife and children.

For a number of years, I tried to talk myself into calling my father or going to see him and asking for forgiveness for all the hate and anger I felt for him. It was extremely challenging to sit down and describe my emotions to share with others. Forgiving my father was the most difficult thing I have ever had to do, because I had to look at myself and chastise myself for allowing this hate to dominate my life for so long.

My father has come to me and said he is proud of the men my brother and I have become, and he admits that although he does not say it enough, he loves us. I decided to take a step to mend fences with my father, so at age 27, I invited him and his wife to Thanksgiving dinner at my house. He said he did not know if they could make it, and he never called back to let me know one way or another. I will continue to do as my mother says and pray for him. I always hoped that maybe one day, my absent father wouldn't be that anymore.

That situation was a major step backward in my efforts to repair my relationship with my father. I had reached out to him, and he kicked me in the gut. It took a lot out of me just to invite him to my house – something I'd never done before. For a few months afterward, I reverted to feeling my father did not care about building a relationship with me. I told myself that forgiving him was going to be a process, and that I needed to take one step at a time. In restoring any relationship, we must always remember we have to invest for the long haul. It did not take one day to destroy that relationship, so it may take years to repair it. If we expect the other person to take as many steps toward us as we do to him or her, we would be waiting for a long time to rebuild that relationship.

I don't just want to educate others about the importance of forgiveness. I want to use this book as another opportunity to let my father know I forgive him and that I am sorry for harboring hate in my heart for him. My heart carried a lot of hate that should not have been there. I think I even allowed the issues with my father to create self-hate and self-doubt in my life. I hated things about myself because I let my father affect me the way he did. I also believe our issues caused me to question my worth when I was growing up.

I wondered why anyone would want to be my friend, since even my own father didn't want to be my friend. I am glad those thoughts never stuck in my head for too long. So many children are not fortunate enough to say that. The father issues haunt them for their entire lives. I decided not to allow that hate to triumph over me any longer.

As I contemplate the hate and anger I had in my heart for my father, I worry about the youth of today and their absent fathers. It is not healthy for young people to grow up with hate simmering inside them. It makes for a less productive and effective person. I want the best for single mothers and fathers, children, and their absent fathers.

This world need more love, and if we can curtail the hate children may have toward their absent fathers, that will help. It is difficult for a seven-year-old boy to discuss his feelings about his absent father. He may not even understand these feelings. He does not know if he loves his father or hates his father. At that age, children internalize their feelings, and that is when the danger zone for hate can start to build. Before you know it, the seven-year-old is fifteen and has a variety of issues that stem from the built-up anger with his absent father.

I am still hurt and a bit angry with my father, but I have decided to help him live the rest of his life knowing his oldest son loves and forgives him. When I talk to him or text with him, I never bring up the past. I am sure that one day, we will discuss it, but at the moment, I want to focus on the future we will have. I just celebrated a birthday two days ago, and historically, my father has always called a couple days after my birthday. He is trying to do much better; in fact, he was the first person to call on my birthday this year. He also said he wants to come down to Tulsa from Oklahoma City more often so he can see his children. I thought that was an honorable thing to say, and I hope he follows through.

I hear many stories about young men not wanting to talk with their fathers. They have so much anger built up, just as I did. Their fathers are in prison, and it may take them years to get out or it may take these young men years to escape their self-imposed prisons of hate and doubt. I want to inspire young men and women to express their anger in a positive way. I want to them to release the anger or hate they have and channel it toward being successful. They can use the dislike of their fathers to push themselves to greatness.

I took the pain, anger, and hate I had for my father and turned it into a book that will hopefully one day speak to thousands of people about my experience. My experiences are no different from that of thousands of young boys and girls. They need to know that just because their fathers are not around, does not mean they cannot be successful in their own lives. They do not have to turn to gangs for acceptance. They can change the world, create the next million-dollar business, invent the next life saving procedure, or inspire countless other young people.

I admit it is difficult for me to forgive my father. Even to this day, I still hold onto some hurt feelings because I think about how my life would have been if my father had been around. But then, I consider the fact that at a certain time in my father's life, he was not capable of being a role model for children. I have to remind myself that my life is a continuous story, and the final chapter has not been written.

Every broken promise, every tear shed, every heart-wrenching moment was supposed to happen to make me a better person. I now have to motivate others whose stories have not reached their final chapters, either, and encourage them to use adversity to propel themselves to greatness. Every great person, every millionaire, every leader of the free world had to go through some form of adversity. The test is how you deal with the adversity. Do you let it define you or do you dominate it? My father deserves my forgiveness, and I hope he feels I deserve his forgiveness for having a strong dislike for him as a child.

My father showed me the type of person I did not want to be. I would have preferred that he show me how to become the man he wanted me to be. I had to become my own man and create my own life. I know I was hard on my father during some attempts he made to communicate with me. At a certain point in my life, I was numb to trying to build a relationship with him, and I would not allow his efforts to gain traction. Even though I was hurt and angry, he did not deserve that, and

I hope he can forgive me for that.

# Chapter Twelve

## Never Let Adversity Keep You Down

Even though I grew up with an absent father, I told myself I could not let that prevent me from being successful. I could have gone down the same road as my father, but I chose to better myself and be a good example for others. I look at the fact that I had an absent father as a blessing, because it forced me to grow up quickly and become responsible. I want people who have similar stories to mine to understand we can make the best out of our bad situations. Too often, young people who have absent fathers go down the wrong road, and never make it back. Writing this story was very therapeutic and allowed me to get some things off my chest. I would advise those in situations like mine to take out time to write down some things that have been on their minds, and they will see how good it makes them feel.

Life is full of challenges; and how you deal with those challenges is up to you. You are the key to your success. No one else should be able to keep you from achieving your dreams. I refused to let my father's absence turn me into a statistic. I wanted to be successful and inspire others to pull themselves up by the bootstraps and achieve their goals. My life has not been easy, but has not been the most difficult life it could have been. Many young people have to grow up without a mother or father; many have a father who is in jail, and the mother has to be both mother and father. And many young people choose the wrong path because they did not have any direction from key leaders in their families or communities.

You have the capacity to create anything you want, but you must be the one to solve your own problems. At no point should you allow what others think of you to define your self-image. You are special as a human being and deserve to be treated that way. Don't allow your inner self to keep you from reaching your full potential. You can be your own worst enemy when it comes to success. How many times have you talked yourself out of doing something that could have propelled you to greatness? I know it is hard to overcome your inner self.

I routinely told myself I was not good enough to be at the same level as some of my peers when I was younger, and this insecurity still affects me to this day. It is a battle I have to fight on a daily basis, as I know most people do. Why shouldn't I get that promotion? Why shouldn't I make as much money as the next guy? I would be a better millionaire than other millionaires! I deserve to have my true talents shine and should not hold myself back.

This is the same thing you must tell yourself. You may find yourself wasting your knowledge, skills, and abilities at your current job or organization. I have seen so many people who have the potential to do great things, but they allow themselves to succeed only at failure.

I have worked in a variety of jobs during my career. I have worked as a cook for an amusement park, a grocery store clerk, a hospice care professional, a mortgage broker, etc. I have had the pleasure of working with hundreds of people, and the one thing I notice is their drive and personality. I have always felt I can teach anyone anything, as long as that person has the right personality and ambition. Successful people have a drive inside of them that never stops.

One of my favorite sayings is that excuses are tools of incompetence used to build monuments of nothingness; those who choose to use them seldom amount to anything. Since hearing that maxim, I have chosen to use it as a motto for my life to keep me on track. We all make excuses on a daily basis. Some excuses are used to explain why we have not accomplished a goal. Others are excuses in our personal lives. We have heard many motivational speakers discuss the importance of not making excuses.

When I started writing this book, I thought about all the excuses my father made on why he was not a part of my life. I also thought about all the excuses I make every day. I had to look myself in the mirror and have a frank conversation with myself. I asked myself why was I not as successful as I wanted to be – not what I thought other people wanted me to be, but what I wanted to be. I have always thought being a millionaire was a mark of a successful person, and I wanted to be a millionaire. I wondered how I would achieve this goal. I have had all kinds of ideas for new businesses, but I have allowed my inner pessimism to keep me from launching any of them. This happens to so many people. There is another saying that the graveyard is the wealthiest place on Earth.

All the ideas, plans, and future millionaires and billionaires lie in those graveyards. I have wanted to write a book since I became an adult, but I had the same problem with it that so many of us have. I wondered, how do I get started? Why would people want to hear what I have to say? How am I going to get people to buy my book?

We can't make ourselves wealthy if we do not first believe in ourselves and try something. We may not succeed on the first venture, but each success or failure can be used to create opportunities for future success. Don't allow yourself to crush your own dreams even before they get started. We are the keys to making our dreams come true. I think about all the people who have died to provide me with the opportunities I have, and I want to make them proud. We are fortunate to have the ability to succeed.

We are blessed beyond measure, and we owe it to everyone who came before us, and who will follow after us, to strive to make our dreams come true. Not everyone wants to become a millionaire. Some just want to become the best teachers they can become, make the best desserts, build the best houses, or make the most unique jewelry. You can be a success at whatever you want, and if you love your craft or talent enough, you can make a living beyond your wildest dreams.

Some of the most influential people in history had to deal with adversity and self doubt. A well-known actress was born to an alcoholic father who was abusive to her mother and sister. Her father left her family when she was four. Her mother raised her and supported her and her sister with her job as a psychiatric nurse. Her mother did not give up on her family. She encouraged her children to be anything they wanted to be. This actress started her career in a movie called, " Jungle Fever." She rose to stardom as a highly talented and beautiful person both on the inside and outside. Her name is Halle Berry.

Halle Berry has always been one of my favorite actresses. She is strong and very talented. I find it interesting that you never know what people go through when they are growing up and even into adulthood. She has had to deal with a lot with men; unfortunately, she's had several marriages that did not work, but she still stays strong and focuses on her children, just like her mother did. From time to time, we mimic our parents. I am sure that Halle's mother is proud that her daughter has been able to focus on her children as she did when she was in a similar situation. Our strong mothers are the key to raising children when their fathers decide to be absent.

Halle has played some very strong roles. She has proved herself to be a fighter who will not allow anything to hold her back. As I think about my daughter and the adversities she will face while growing up, I wonder how she will combat them. Halle's father was not there for her. He did not walk her down the isle. He did not wipe her tears when she cried. He missed the most important parts of her life. So who loses in that situation? They both do.

What would have happened if her father did not become an alcoholic and decided to be a present father? How would both of their lives evolved? He could have been by her side as she received some of her awards. He could have been on the set with her and helped her rehearse her lines. That is what a real father does.

We miss so much in our children's lives, sometimes by being selfish and not wanting to take responsibility. Halle did not allow the adversity of having an absent father affect her. She is a success and she is working to ensure that her children are, as well – just like so many mothers and fathers across the world.

Another influential person grew up thinking his grandparents were his parents and that his mother was his sister. He is a famous singer who has performed for millions of people. He is the only person to be inducted into the Rock ‘n’ Roll Hall of Fame three times. His father left his mother before he was born. Fortunately, his mother had a great support system to help her raise her child. His mother saw that he loved to play the guitar, so she supported his dream of becoming a blues player. This famous musician is Eric Clapton. Eric, like me, had a strong influence from his grandparents.

# Chapter Thirteen

## A Letter to My Mother

"Mother, with unconditional love, you gave up a large piece of your youth to raise my brother and me. I can never repay you for all the things you did for me. I can only promise that I will do my best to make you proud. I want you to look at me and say, 'That's my son and I am so proud of the man he has become.' I promised myself when I was a boy that I would be successful and make sure you are taken care of, no matter what. I am not there yet, but I promise I will be that successful man you wanted me to be. I have taken what you have taught me and I have tried to apply it to my life. "I have tried all my life to do things differently from my absent father, but I found that I have made the same types of decisions he has made. When I look in the mirror some days, I feel so disappointed at the man I have become."

"I have lied, cheated, hurt people, and been selfish. You did not raise me to be the way I am. You raised me to respect women and treat people the best I can. I have tried to be there for as many people as I can, like you would have wanted me to, but I have still negatively affected too many people."

"As I write this letter, tears fall as I acknowledged to myself I have not grown to be the man I need to be. I do know what I need to do to get better, and I promise you I will be better. I have almost lost you twice, and before death has another chance, I will make you smile. You have told me how proud you are of the men my brother and I have become, but I feel I have so much left to do to become who I am supposed to be. You have taught me to be independent, strong, entrepreneurial, and a leader. Mother, your little boy is growing up to be a man."

"Even with an absent father, I have been able to graduate from high school, college, and graduate school. I will be a role model for other people to let them know they can do anything they can dream of. I will not let the pain he caused by leaving keep me from fulfilling my destiny. I love you, Mother. I am glad God blessed me and millions of children with strong, independent mothers. I know that as a child, I may have been a bit difficult. I know you were in labor with me for 35 hours, struggling to bring me into this world, and I thank you for that. I owe any success I have to you and your hard work.

"I remember the 12- to 16-our workdays you endured just so my brother and I could have the best you could provide. I think about all the young children who are not fortunate enough to have a loving and caring mother. They do not get to experience the love of a mother. You have been my role model since I was a young child."

"I saw how you spoke with people, helped them, and encouraged them. There is a reason we could never go out of the house without your running into someone who you knew. You sacrificed so much for my brother and me to have a normal life. I appreciate your being hard on us sometimes, because you had to do your best to teach us how to be men."

"Being the child of an entrepreneur is a huge benefit to me. I learned so much about running a business from watching you. I know you made mistakes and learned along the way, but you stayed strong and did not allow anything to hold you back. You took us to your hair shows so we could see how entrepreneurship worked. We got to watch you network, prepare, and execute your plans. Many young girls have grown up to be great successes because you counseled them while doing their hair. You are my leader, my inspiration, and my motivator. Thank you for everything you have done in my life. I can never repay or thank you enough."

# Chapter Fourteen

## Father,

## I Forgive You

I have been through so many emotions during my 35 years, but I am excited about the years to come. I started writing this book as a way to release the hate I had for my absent father. I promised myself to let all the hurt, pain, and disappointment go as I began writing this book eight years ago. I told my wife that and she said, "Well, it just took time for things to go full circle." I agree with her, because eight years ago, this book would have been completely different. I am sure it would have been more negative and not as positive. My relationship with my father was worse eight years ago, and I was a different person then, too. As we age or experience more things, our perspective changes.

Over the past few years, my relationship with my father has improved. He has been making an effort to reach out not only to me, but also to his other children. I am proud of what he has been doing. I think he is still trying to figure out how to build relationships. In 2015, he spent his first Christmas in 30 years with one of his daughters. He has seen both of my children a few times. We still don't have the type of relationship wherein we call each other weekly, but we have more regular contact than we have had in the past. My uncle Sylvester is extremely happy that my father and I are building a better relationship.

Last year was the first time I ever took my father out to dinner for Father's Day. It felt good to spend time with him. We have a lot in common when it comes to our love for sports, so our conversation was mostly focused on that. We were able to go to a barbecue place with a number of TVs with sporting events on them, so that was great. That was what I wanted for years, but because of pride on both sides, I did not take the opportunity. I want a better relationship with my father. He is getting older and I want him to know I love him. He says he loves me when we communicate, and even though I am older, it still is good to hear from my father.

When I started writing this book, I was in a bad place mentally. I knew I wanted to be successful, but I felt I could not truly be successful until I let go of all the anger in my life. I knew I was trapped by the anger. I have heard if you want to get something off your chest, it is always best to write it down. In this instance, I decided my story was so similar to that of thousands of boys and girls that I had to share it with them.

My father made a number of mistakes as a young man, as many men have made, but I hope people did not hold against me things I did when I was younger, either. He deserved my forgiveness. He is my father and I will always honor him. Every day is a journey, and I hope he and I can enjoy this journey together.

If you have a child who has no relationship with his or her father, it is important to handle the conversations as my mother did. She never bashed my father. She consistently asked us to pray for him, as she did. If the absent father is only absent because you, as the mother, are mad at him and you do not want to let him see his children, you should reconsider your emotions. Forgive him, pray for him, and share your children with him. It may take years, but it is worth it for the children's sakes. The father must be willing to cooperate, so to the fathers out there, it is imperative that you step back into your children's lives. Don't just be part-time dads. Teach your children what is right and what is wrong. Don't be a stranger to your own blood. The situation in which you conceived a child may be less than optimal, but your children did not ask to be born into a negative situation.

I know some of you absent fathers use their financial instability as an excuse, but allow the fact that you have a child or children to push you to strive for success. Go back to school and get your degree or a trade. Admit to your child's mother that you want to be a better person, and ask her if she can help you do that. She may hate you for the things you have done in the past, but take on that challenge and win her over with your actions.

Be there for your children. We need you fathers in our lives. The tears I shed while growing up, and during writing this book, are the same tears thousands of innocent boys and girls shed on a daily basis. Break the curse of absent fathers by making the commitment to be a present father.

To a woman, I say this: If you are dating a man who is not in the best place right now, think about protecting yourself. Take birth control and keep condoms on you at all time if you are going to be sexually active. In order to create more present fathers, it is going to take women and men who make better decisions.

If you are dating someone and he can't even take care of himself, how is he going to take care of you and your child? I never understood when I was younger why girls seemed attracted to the thugs or bad boys, but as I got older, it made sense. Girls do pursue those types of males when they are younger but when they get older, possibly after having a child or two, then they wanted to be with a shirt and tie type of guy, like me. This is not always the case. Some women prefer a man with a rough side. I know plenty of men who people would consider a thug who are stepping up and taking care of their children.

Another way we are going to break the curse is to educate ourselves. The better-educated men and women we have, the more responsible we will be about taking care of children who are conceived. Now I know people with college educations do sometimes become absent fathers, but the hope is that the more women and men focus on their education and becoming successful, the less likely they will be to have children early in life before they complete their education. Hopefully they will have a better chance of getting married or in a committed relationship first if they wait until they have reached some of their educational and career goals.

Some people may read this book and feel it does not apply to them, and indeed, it may not. But I invite you to take the knowledge shared in this book and either apply it to your own life or share it with someone you know. The suggestions I've offered in this book do not constitute a silver bullet to fix all issues with mothers and fathers. I wanted to share a story with which many children and parents will identify, and provide a few ideas on how to help with a few situations my readers may be dealing with.

My absent father is trying to be more present recently. We mainly text each other, but it is a step forward in our relationship. I want the best for my father, and I know he wants the best for me. He helped bring me into the world, and I can never thank him enough for that. I had so much anger toward my father, and I am glad that I started writing this book. So many people out there hold onto anger toward something or someone. I am an example of how letting go of that anger helps make you a better person. If you have a grudge or anger toward your father, mother or anyone else, write your feelings down and try to forgive. It is very difficult, and it will require baby steps, but you can do it. Even if you do not feel like you can be around the person yet, it still helps you to forgive.

I do not consider myself a saint, and I hope my family can forgive me for any problems I may cause in the future. I want to look into my children's eyes and let them know I am human, but I want to be the best human I can be for them. My father and I have not had the conversation about how I have felt my entire adult life. I do not know that we will ever have that conversation. I also do not know how he will react to this book. My father is a very prideful person and he does not take criticism well. I can only hope this book will bring us even closer, although I think initially, he may be a bit upset. My goal is for my father to tour with me during my speaking engagements so he may offer some insight into the mind of an absent father. That is a tall order for anyone, and I do not know if my father is up to that challenge. I know there are so many people who would love to hear his side of the story and possibly get answers to questions they have about their own absent fathers.

I forgive my father for being absent. My previous hate for him could not bring back any birthdays he missed. It could not bring back any missed events or dry any tears. I had to grow up with an absent father. But I told myself, "Get over it and enjoy your life." After all, I am not the only person to grow up with an absent father, but I have to strive for success and set an example for other children who grew up with absent fathers. Growing up with an absent father doesn't have to identify you or define you. You can look at that as an opportunity to prove you will not be a statistic and you will succeed at achieving your goals.

So many men and women in prisons never knew their fathers. Their fathers were not there to discipline them. Their fathers were not there to give them love. Their fathers were not there to help mold them to becoming productive adults. That is no excuse for not achieving success, but you need support to help you along. It is time to take your adversities and turn them around to your achievements. We cannot make our fathers be present, but what we can do is ensure that the next generations of children with absent fathers enjoy the love of people who care for them and have positive male and female role models.

I thank the God above for allowing me to be an example for others. I also thank him for everything he has done for my friends, my family, and me. My earthly father is responsible for my being here right now, and I love him for that. I also love him for trying to form a better relationship with me and my other siblings. He is getting older, but I think he is becoming wiser and understands that he needs to connect with his children. I am not going to beat him down about what he didn't do for me in the past. Instead, I am going to cherish the future we will have together. Some people are not able to build relationships with their fathers because those men have passed on or are locked up.

I am blessed to have a second chance to build a relationship with my father. I hope you all take the same opportunity and make the best out of the rest of the time you have with your absent fathers. Sometimes the child has to be the bigger person to forgive and start rebuilding a relationship with the absent father. Take the first step and forgive. The rest of your life will soar beyond measure. Encourage love over hate.

# Chapter Fifteen

## How to Explain an Absent Father to My Child

My mother never said anything bad about my absent father. She always advised my brother and me to pray for him. That's the best advice I can give a mother with a child who has an absent father. Men are not perfect, and neither are women. We all make mistakes and need forgiveness at some point. The issues with absent fathers have been going on for thousands of years, and children have been getting their hearts broken the same about of time.

Too often are single mothers left to explain to their children why their fathers are absent. Also too often are the single mothers required to be the mothers, fathers, and grandfathers. In many families, not only is the father not in the picture, but also the grandfather is not active in the children's lives, either. It is important to have stable men in the family. My father was not around when I was growing up, but thankfully, I had my grandfathers and uncles to help fill the void. Not all children are so fortunate.

So how do you have the conversation with your children when they start asking questions about where their father is? Just remember this discussion is very important and could affect your children for the rest of their lives. If a child feels he is the reason the father left, he may become withdrawn or have further issues as he grows into an adult. The first step is to ask them why they think their father is not around as much as they would like. This will give you an idea what your child is thinking and you will know how to proceed.

If your child says he does not know, you have a clean slate to discuss this topic. If your child gives a specific reason as to why he thinks his father is not around, you need to tailor your message to carefully respond to this. Just keep in mind that your child is impressionable and will trust anything you say, to a certain extent. If you are dealing with a toddler, your message is going to be different than if you are dealing with a pre-teen. I feel it is important to tell children the truth, depending on what that truth is. It is difficult to tell a child his father is in prison, but if that's the case, you should explain that the father is in prison, and that's a place you never want the child to go. Emphasize the importance of education as a means of staying out of prison or other trouble.

I also believe if a child's father or mother is in prison, the remaining parent must offer to take the child to visit the imprisoned parent. I know some think the child should not see his parent like that, but this situation can be used as a teachable moment by once again focusing on the importance of education and striving for success. Even though the other parent may have done something wrong, he still has the right to see his child.

Some people will say if that parent wanted to see the child, he would not have engaged in behavior that got him arrested. Once again, we all make mistakes. That being said, if you feel the imprisoned parent will be negative or that he or she doesn't appreciate the time with the child, don't take the child. That parent is going to have to earn your trust that he or she will not inflict additional damage.

If the father is not around because he just doesn't want to make time for your child, that conversation can be difficult as well. The first conversation with the father should help you get an idea of how much he wants to be in the life of the child. Don't let him off the hook. Hold him to a schedule and remind him if he does not follow that schedule, but do not nag. If he does not want anything to do with you or the child, let him know he will nevertheless have to be financially responsible for the child, but that you will never say anything bad about him to your child. Let him know your child will grow up and make up his own mind whether he wants a relationship with his father, who will by that time be getting older and needing someone to love him.

If the child's father is not going to be around, make sure to tell the child his father was trying to figure some things out in his life, and at this point, he has decided not be around as much as you would like, but that you will all pray for him. Allow this conversation to be a teachable moment, too, and show your child the importance of praying for someone and not hating another person.

Your prayers that he will choose to be in his child's life may not come to fruition quickly, but it is important for your child to see that you are the bigger person and that you show love and compassion. You may not know it, but your children may mimic the way you handle situations for years.

I know it was difficult for my mother to always be positive about my father, but she always told us, "You will make up your own mind about your father. Just pray for him." It is tough to speak in a positive way about someone when he is paying $365 per month to take care of two or three children. It is also difficult if the father never gives Christmas or birthday gifts, or forgets to attend important academic or sporting events.

My mother will tell you she is not a saint, but she felt in her heart that she would rather her boys have a positive picture of their father than a negative one. I can never thank my mother enough for that, because that built the foundation for my father and I to have a better relationship. Mothers are special in the sense that they can take so much and still be positive and loving. I know many single mothers who are raising their children with minimal help, yet they keep their focus on their children.

Another important element to consider when discussing an absent father is your opinion about him personally, and how you feel about his not being there. It is important that you are not blaming yourself. Your child can sense when something is wrong or if you are not happy. A key requirement for successfully raising your child is to take time to focus on yourself and your happiness. If you are not happy with yourself, you will take that unhappiness out on your children. How many of us have been having a bad day and snapped at our children for minor offenses that would normally have been swept under the rug?

My mother was never a fan of bringing a lot of men around the house. She knew she was a mother first, and there are times when she would put her romantic relationships on hold to nurture her relationship with my brother and me. I know that you have to live your life and that you have needs, but when you bring a man into the picture, it should only be when you are serious about him.

If you are dating casually, it is a good idea to do so away from the eyes of your child. You are first and foremost a mother or father, responsible for raising your child in the best manner possible. This is difficult for a woman or men who do not have a village to help when you need that night out, but just remember, your children will be better off in the long run.

If anything, have the guy or lady come over while the kids are sleep. Focus on your own happiness, and be aware that a man or woman may not be what makes you happy. Some women and men benefit from taking a break from dating and focusing on things that make them happy, such as furthering their education, creating a business, or starting a hobby.

# Chapter Sixteen

## My Village

I've talked several times about my village or individuals who were important in my development. I firmly believe the single mothers and fathers need a village to help raise their children. When I was a child, most weekends, I went to my great-grandparents' house and spent time with them. My village included a number of people who helped mold me into the adult I have become. But there were others, too: my Nanny, my uncle Billy, my neighborhood friend Kevin, and my grandfather David.

My "second" mother I call "Nanny," but her real name was Lucinda Wells was such an important person in my life. She was my great-grandmother, but I always thought it was odd that my Nanny was really my grandmother's mother. I do not know why that was so hard for me to grasp. I think it was because of the way my grandmother used to speak to my Nanny. It seemed like she was the mother instead of the child. Nanny was raped as a young girl while she was staying with her father's friend when he was on the road, preaching. I did not learn about this until I was in my mid-twenties. She and her father decided not to press charges on his friend's son. Out of that horrible situation came a blessing, which was my grandmother. It is amazing what you learn when you start to gather information about your history. If it hadn't been for that violent act, I may not be here today. That is crazy!

I started spending the weekends with Nanny when I was in middle school, because my mother worked long hours. My mother would take me to Nanny's house either Friday night or early Saturday morning. It was interesting being a rambunctious little boy and hanging out with my great-grandmother. I have fond memories of Nanny. She was the first person who showed me the importance of home-cooked meals. She was old school and she did not believe in wasting any food. She made the best hamburgers! She would swirl butter in a pan and brown my hamburger buns. To this day, I cannot eat a burger unless the buns are toasted. She made sure I was respectful and appreciated learning. She frequently asked me to fetch one of the volumes of an encyclopedia and read from it.

I loved spending the weekends with Nanny and her husband, Hardy, whom we called Grandpa Hardy. I loved my great-grandparents. They taught me the importance of homemade foods, treating people right, history, and how to be a good son. I remember that they grew cotton. I had always heard about slaves having to pick cotton, but I did not know how hard it was until Grandpa Hardy took me outside one day and told me we would be picking cotton.

I was excited, but it was so hot to have to work outside. I was about nine years old, but I remember it like it was yesterday. He grabbed a couple of bags and started showing me how to pick cotton. He was good at picking it, but I was not. The cotton pricked my fingers. He said I needed to understand how difficult it was for slaves to pick cotton. We had to separate the seeds from the cotton. It was a great experience for me. He was another great male influence.

One of the most memorable things I learned was that President Woodrow Wilson was on the $100,000 dollar bill, and I also learned about different dinosaurs and sharks. I remember wondering why was President Wilson so important to be on such a high dollar bill. Nanny and I were attached at the hip. She took me everywhere with her. She did not drive, but she would run her errands with her best friend, who still drove at that time. Her friend's endearing name for me was "Pistol Pete."

As my Nanny got older, her memory faded. She was

no longer able to stay at home by herself because she had developed dementia. She spent her last 10 years in a nursing home. I have many regrets about this time in her life. Early on, when Nanny was placed in the nursing home, I did not go see her regularly. I was selfish and did not want to see her in there. It didn't occur to me that she probably did not want to be in there. She was lonely, because people can't understand losing their memory unless it is happening to them.

I think back on how much joy I could have brought her by just being there for her, like she was for me. I never even took my girlfriend - now my wife - to see her. I robbed my Nanny and my wife from the opportunity to know each other. During the last three years of her life, I did visit her more. I worked for a hospice company, and Nanny's nursing home was one of my accounts. I was able to go by a few times a week to wheel her up and down the hall as I spoke with her.

During her final days, I was by her side. Right before she died, the nurse called me to let me know she felt Nanny would pass soon. I rushed up to the nursing home, and she passed shortly after I got there. I remember sitting in the room with just her and me after she was gone. It was the end of a life that meant so much to me. She was my best friend and my second mother. Even as I write these words, tears come to my eyes, because I miss Nanny. I know she is looking down, and I want to make her proud.

My village also included my mother's brother, William (Billy) Butler. I had five uncles on my mother's side of the family. They were all great, but I gravitated to my Uncle Billy the most. He was hilarious. We had a great bond and relationship. He was the uncle who would joke around the most, so to a young kid, that is perfect. Every time I saw him, he brought a smile to my face. One of the favorite family stories is about my Uncle Billy and me.

I believe I was about eight years old and we had been playing around all day. He had told me his foot was hurt and that I had to be careful around it. Well, of course, when my mother told me it was time to go, I made the dumb decision to purposely jump up and step on his foot. I knew I could outrun my uncle, so I hit the door and dashed towards the car. Before I even got off the porch, my uncle grabbed me, yanked me up in the air, and whipped my butt. I was so hurt that my uncle had disciplined me. It was the first time he ever had to do that. I told him I was sorry, and we moved on, being best buddies again.

My uncle married a nice lady who we called, Aunt Linda, who lived across the street from my grandmother. She had a son who was close to my age. My uncle often came and picked me up so I could hang out with him and his new stepson Rick. I built a great relationship with my new cousin, and with my uncle, we were like the three amigos. He served as a father figure as well, by being present when I needed him. He was always available to help me with my car if I needed it.

I could talk to him about everyday issues. He had a way of making you laugh, even when you did not want to laugh. He was a special person to our family. My uncle had a genuine interest in my success. He would come to my games and support my ideas. He was also a great cook, and he taught me about the importance of using spices. As I got older, I thought he and I would go into a food business together.

About six years ago, my uncle was diagnosis with prostate cancer. This is a form of cancer that is prevalent in black men, and it is treatable with early detection. Like many black men, my uncle did not have his prostate exam as regularly as he needed. When my mother told me my uncle had cancer, I immediately broke down. I was working in the hospice industry at the time, and I knew how cancer could affect someone.

My uncle went through treatments, but he did not have the money or the insurance to get effective treatment. He enrolled into an experimental treatment program with a local hospital. I tried my best to see my uncle as much as possible, because I did not know how long I would have with him. I thought he was getting better, because he never spoke about the cancer in a negative way. After a few weeks, though, I noticed he was losing weight and he did not have an appetite. One of my aunts moved in to help take care of him. She called me one day and told me my uncle had been transported to the hospital. When I got there, the doctor told me my uncle had end-stage prostate cancer and that he had less than six months to live.

My heart sank. I walked in and talked to my uncle. I asked him how he was doing and what the doctor had said. He told me he could not feel his legs, so he had to come to the hospital. During our conversation, he said he saw a little angel in the corner of the room. That terrified me. I knew hallucinations were an effect of medication and disease processes from my training with hospice. Even though I had the knowledge for working in these types of scenario, when it is your own family, it is difficult.

During his hospital stay, the doctor told us we would have to take him home on hospice. This was agonizing because I knew it meant my uncle was probably not going to get better. I asked myself how long he would have that Eddie Murphy laugh and that infectious smile. How long would my uncle live? My aunt and I got him home with all his equipment he would need. Then I had a very important conversation with my uncle. I asked him if he understood his prognosis. He told me he did. He told me he wanted me to take charge of all decision-making, including his finances.

He may not have known it, but he made me the proudest person on the Earth. For someone to entrust his or her final decisions to you is an immeasurable sign of trust. I was honored because he had siblings and children who could have done this. I told my uncle I would take care of everything.

As the family prepared for the expected death of my uncle, we met with a funeral home director my mother knew. She laid out the financial responsibilities for the funeral. I was amazed at how much funerals cost. We had two options: We could bury him or cremate him. I knew my uncle did not want to be cremated because he had told me that in earlier conversations.

Besides, I did not want to cremate my uncle. Unfortunately, my uncle had allowed his life insurance to lapse. He also had very little money, as he had not been working regularly. Everyone in the family was at this meeting, and no one had the money to foot the bill of a traditional funeral. To this day, I feel horrible that I was not financially stable enough bury my uncle.

We went home that night and prepared for a family dinner. We planned to explain the options to my uncle. I assumed his brothers and sisters would want to have the conversation with him, but none of them did. I started getting upset because I felt it was their duty to discuss this situation with their brother. They walked around the apartment for hours. Eventually, my mother went up to my aunt and me and asked, "Are one of you going to talk to him about this?" My aunt looked at me. I was so frustrated that I said, "I will have the talk with him," and I walked into his room to begin the most difficult discussion I had ever had.

It was just my uncle and I in the room. I once again reminded him he might not be with us long. My tears started to flow like waterfalls, but I kept talking. I told him I wanted to speak with him about his final wishes. I told him we met with a funeral company that would bury him once he passed. He looked right at me the entire time and did not shed one tear. I thought he was the bravest man I had ever known. He looked death in the face and stood strong.

I told my uncle a lie that has haunted me to this day: I told him we would not cremate him. I showed him the prices of each option, and said I planned to raise the money to pay for his funeral. I just could not bear for my uncle to think about being cremated when he was already dealing with so much. After that conversation, I had a new respect for my uncle. Now even though I told him that I would not cremate him, I knew it was the decision I would have to make. The family supported me in my decision, because they knew the finances were not there for any other option. And even to cremate my uncle, we would still have to pay for those services. I made the decision that we would liquidate everything he had to help pay for the funeral. We were able to get the money needed for the service.

I miss my uncle terribly. It still seems unreal that he passed in 2011. A piece of my heart was taken when he died. I am glad I was able to have the time with him. That process turned me into a stronger man. He helped mold me into a better adult by showing me love and being present when I needed him. Uncle, you will be missed.

Kevin Kelly is an important figure in my life. I met Kevin when I was a young boy living in condos called Florence Park. He has a daughter, Kendra who is close to my age. She and I started playing around with the other neighborhood kids. We ended up establishing a great friendship. I got to meet her father, Kevin, one day while we were playing, and I thought he was so cool and funny.

As we grew older, my brother and I would spend more time with Kevin and Kendra. My mom loved Kevin. She felt he was great with kids and was funny, too. We would spend hours with them. His condo became the neighborhood hangout. He was a drummer, so he had a drum set, movies, food, a piano, and eight tracks. We never played with the eight tracks, but it was fun to know someone who had them.

The reason I decided to write about Kevin is because he was very important to my childhood. He is a white man who is old enough to be my father, but he was like a big brother to me. Not many young black boys have such a close relationship with an older white man. Our relationship was special because it proved to me it was OK to have a close friend of a different race. I had already had good relationships with the other kids in the neighborhood who were mostly white, but I had never before been close to an older white male.

Kevin treated my brother and me as if we were his sons. He took us to baseball games, restaurants, and other exciting places. This was a new experience for us because, for the most part, our uncles did not take us out to fun places like Kevin. The only uncle who did that at the time was my Uncle Sylvester. Kevin never made us feel we were less worthy than the other kids in the neighborhood. He appreciated our love for his daughter and enjoyed seeing her when she came down for the summers and school breaks.

As I became a young adult, I had more interactions with white males, and my relationship with Kevin was the impetus for that. I feel it is important to ensure children and young adults are around people of as many different races as possible. They need to learn that all people something special about them, no matter what they look like, whom they pray to, or what sexual orientation they have.

I saw Kevin a few weeks ago after his hip surgery. It had been a while since I had seen him, and I took my children to meet him. He was just as nice to them as he was to us when we were growing up. He told his daughter Kendra to take them into the other room and let them play on his drums. That was so fun for them. When I am with Kevin and Kendra, I don't think about race, because we have never let that divide us. We see each other as family whom we love.

Kendra was so nice to my two children, and they just fell in love with her. They were not too fond of her cat, but they got used to it after a while. I can never thank Kevin and Kendra enough for allowing me into their lives and loving me for who I am.

Finally, I must describe my grandfather, David Carolina. He was the funniest man I have ever known. He was lived in Moffett, Oklahoma, the entire time I knew him. My mother tells a story of when I first met my grandfather. She said I was still a baby, and when he saw me, he took my elbow and matched it up to my mother's and my father's elbows. He was old school, so I guess that was his mystical way of seeing if I really belonged to my father. I can imagine, with having 19 kids, my grandfather had a number of women claiming his sons had fathered their children. The elbow test did not sit well with my mother. She got upset, but his charm calmed her down.

My grandfather was a mechanic and a man of minimal needs. He had a small, two-bedroom house next door to my Uncle Sylvester. One of the most interesting things I remember about my grandfather is that he ate breakfast at 3 p.m. every day. To a young boy, that is odd; I wanted to eat at a normal time. He would fix us something to eat, but he himself would not eat until 3 p.m.

He was also the mayor of Moffett for over 10 years. He had the ability to talk to anyone. I often rode with him as he made his rounds, and everyone waved and came up to his car to talk, and he always got out to visit people in their homes. He was truly the people's mayor. One of his major accomplishments was getting paved roads for the town.

My grandfather taught me the importance of being respectful and working hard. It was great to see him and observe how excited he was to see my brother and me. He loved us and wanted the best for us. I remember just siting on the back porch swing and enjoying the weather. He also let us help him spray diesel fuel around his house to keep the wasps away. To this day, I think using diesel fuel as a bug repellant is strange, but it worked.

My grandfather was a great role model for me. He felt it was important to treat people with respect and welcome them as guests when they came to his home. He made sure that when my brother and I stayed over, we had a comfortable place to sleep. Dipping tobacco was his daily activity. I remember one day by brother kept bothering him to give him some of his tobacco. In my brother's defense, the tobacco did look like a brownie. My grandfather kept telling him no until he broke down and said, "OK... here! My brother took a bite and almost threw up on the spot. My grandfather said, "You better not throw up in this living room; go in the restroom. "That was the funniest thing ever. Needless to say, my brother never asked for my grandfather's tobacco again.

Having a relationship with my grandfather was important to me. I do not remember us ever talking about the relationship, or lack thereof, with my father. My grandfather wanted his son to do right by us, but he never criticized him in my presence. His willingness to step up and help take care of my brother and me really meant a great deal to us. We couldn't wait to see our grandfather.

I am thankful I did not have an Absent Grandfather to go along with my absent father. So many young boys and girls are being robbed of the opportunity to get to know their grandfathers, and it breaks my heart that our children do not really have a relationship with my wife's father or my father. I know it bothers my wife as well. I think that is why I try to be the best father as I can; I want my children to know the love of their father. I know I need to do a better job of taking my children around my father and Qianna's father, because I know the importance of having a relationship with a grandfather.

When my grandfather passed, I was in college and it was finals week. My mother would not allow me to leave school to come down to Moffett to see my grandfather. She said he would have wanted me to stay in school and focus on my education.

My grandfather wanted nothing more than for me to get an education, because he knew of all the sacrifices that were made for me to be there. I was hurt because I was not at his side during his last breath, but I was comforted to know he wanted me to succeed, and he knew the only way was for me to get an education. I miss him so much. When I go back to Moffett to visit my Uncle Sylvester, I still feel like I am going to see my grandfather walking out of the garage, covered in oil. I know he looks down on me and keeps me safe and focused on success.

# Chapter Seventeen

## Happy Days

The grand finale comes with a release anger, guilt, and pain. Our family has made it through so many obstacles and we look forward to the future My brother has proposed to his girlfriend and they plan to marry in 2017. He is working two jobs to try to prepare for the wedding and provide a great future for his wife. I cannot be more proud of the young man he has become. He did not allow the fact that our father was not an active part of our lives to keep him from striving to be successful.

My brother is a college graduate and has great ideas about being an entrepreneur one day. I commend him because he has not shown the anger toward my father that I did. He graduated with a degree in hotel and restaurant management. He has aspirations of starting his own baking company, featuring unique pastries. My brother has also refused to be cursed by his absent father, and his refusal will push him to achieve his goals. I have no doubt he will be extremely successful.

I think back to when he was a young boy, full of energy. All I wanted for my brother was for him to grow up to be successful. I was so fearful he would end up going down the wrong road. My goal was to try to be the best role model possible so he would see my actions and mimic them. He has become his own man, and I couldn't be prouder of the man he has become. I look forward to seeing him continually grow. He has so many exciting achievements coming soon in his future.

Our mother is also doing great things in her life. After being a single mother since she was 21 years old, she has now been married for seven years to a wonderful man who loves her. She has always been my entrepreneurial inspiration. I wanted to own a business just like she does. She has now started a new venture. She is designing beautiful jewelry for men and women, and I am truly inspired by her. Having my brother and me altered her life, but she did not allow having a baby at 21 stop her from getting a bachelor's degree in arts and science, focusing on cosmetology. She refused to be a statistic and she has inspired and mentored hundreds of young women.

My mother's passion for cosmetology is evident by the hard work she still puts into her craft. Even though she has started a new venture, she continues to take on clients who need their hair styled. I am amazed at her work ethic. She is an active member of her church, she is present in her grandchildren's lives, she volunteers, and she still is the glue that keeps our family together.

When my grandmother passed, my mother assumed the role of keeping everyone in line in the family. She has been a motivating force for our family to stay together and be in one another's lives.

If it weren't for my mother, our family would not be as strong as it is now. Of course, every family has its problems, but I feel my mother is the one to whom everyone turns to help with any conflicts or issues. She has handled her role with grace.

Now that my mother has grandchildren, she is even happier with life. She sees herself in her grandchildren, and that makes her smile. One of my aspirations was to have children with a great wife so my mother could experience the joys of being a grandparent. It is amazing how her eyes light up when she sees our children. I know she was nervous with all the problems we had getting pregnant, but she was supportive every step of the way. She was also present at doctor's appointments for both children during our pregnancies. She wanted to make sure we knew that she loved us and she supported us.

I am interested to see what the future holds for my mother. I see her jewelry business doing great things for her because it is so unique and classy. Teaching and speaking also could be in her future. She would be great at it. She has shown interest in writing a book, and I am going to keep motivating her to do that so we can both travel to spread our messages.

My mother will always be in the lives of my children. She still reminds me to pray for my father, and I feel it is so generous of her to do that. She continues to be my rock and my inspiration for striving to be successful. I intend to help take care of her one-day so she does not have a want in the world that I cannot give her.

Finally, my life is amazing. I could not have imagined I would write a book and actually publish it. If it weren't for my friend Avery, I may still just have this book sitting on the hard drive of my computer with the 18 pages I had written. I am thankful for his believing in me enough to push me to complete this book. My goal is to continue writing books, speaking all over the world, volunteering my time in communities, and providing a great life for my family. I have taken to entrepreneurship, just as my mother has.

In 2011, I started my own food enterprise called Carolina Food Company, LLC. My flagship product was a wine jelly called Toasted Wine Fruit Spreads. It is a mixture of real fruit and real wine to form a jelly product. My grandmother use to make jelly, and she would always try to get me to learn her recipe, but at the time, I was a teenager and more interested in eating the jelly instead of making it. She passed away without anyone in our family learning her jelly recipe.

I was inspired about six years ago to start making jelly that would have made her proud. I developed Toasted Wine Fruit Spreads, and I think she would have loved the product. Since first developing the wine jelly, I have concocted several recipes from a wine-flavored coffee/tea syrup, a wine-flavored pasta sauce, and a line of gourmet dry mixes and dips. Toasted products are now sold in close to 60 locations in Oklahoma and Arkansas.

I am also working on various ventures, including designing a baby tent for the past two years. It is called The Pop-Up Tot. It is designed to be a baby sensory play tent, with other features such as a shade tent, a baby sleeping tent, a diaper changing tent, and a toddler play tent. I hope The Pop-Up Tot will be sold worldwide to families.

I have never created a physical product like The Pop-Up Tot. It has been an interesting experience to learn how to create the product, and conduct the industry and legal research, plus customer testing. My wish is that I can create products, write books, and sell food items for the rest of my life and that I will be able to leave my children with all the tools and finances to be successful.

My hard work is intended to help better their lives in the future. I also want my wife to live the confortable life she deserves. She has been by my side during all my crazy business ideas, and she never discouraged me from striving to reach my goals. That is amazing to me. I hope to show her that her dedication to my dreams and me will pay off one day. This book is another opportunity at success, and she has been there with me in planning from the very beginning.

I am proud to be able to finally finish this book. I feel my last 35 years have prepared me to share my story with the world. I can only hope this book is read by the people who need to hear its message. There are so many young boys and girls who are struggling with the same issues I had, growing up with absent fathers. I want to help as many people as possible. I look forward to future books and speaking opportunities to share my story even further.

# Chapter Eighteen

## The 10-Minute Conversation:

## I Finally Told My Father About This Book

Writing *The Absent Father* has been an amazing journey of emotions and realizations. I have cried, laughed, gasped in amazement, and now completed my first book. I have received immense support and motivation during the writing and editing process. Scores of people have shared their personal stories about their absent and present fathers. Hearing these stories of heartache and triumph have inspired me to complete this book and push my message to as many people as possible. I hope to reach thousands of people with this message of forgiveness.

My father is a man to whom I have been compared for most of my life. He has attributes that I appreciate his passing down to me. I do not know if I hadn't taken the leap of sharing my thoughts and personal story with others whether I would have been able to forgive my father in the way I did. As I have shared the idea of why I started writing this book with others, I have explained to them the way to heal is to forgive. Forgiving has been one of the most difficult actions I have ever had to complete, but it has been one of the most fulfilling.

Many of my friends who knew I was writing this book asked me if I had spoken to my father about it.

They wanted to know what I thought his reaction would be. I let them know I had not discussed the book with him. I think my main reason for not telling my father about the book early on was fear. When I initially started writing, I wanted to put down my thoughts on paper as a way to heal and forgive. I did not plan to share the writing with the world. I thought that if I wrote down my thoughts as I would in a journal, I could stop suppressing my fears, negative feelings, and insecurities.

In giving advice to those with whom I have spoken about forgiveness, I have explained the importance of writing down thoughts and possibly solutions to the problems they are having. That strategy helped push me to write this book. If a process helps me, it may help others, too, so I feel compelled to share my process of healing and forgiveness.

I was extremely nervous about how I would have the discussion with my father about this book. I felt he would be upset with me and that our relationship would be affected by the words I had written. In my mind, he is not the type of man to take criticism or feedback very well. My plan was to write a majority of the book and then speak to him face to face about its contents.

I finally had that conversation with my father. He called me and we started discussing this book. I shared information with him that I had never shared before. I let him know that I started writing a book in 2008 to facilitate the healing and forgiving process, because I had so much hate in my heart for him. I could tell he was taken aback by my comment. I continued discussing my feelings with him. I let him know I was hurt at the fact that he was not an active part of my life while I was growing up, and that my mother had to struggle to raise my brother and me.

I explained that I felt I was imprisoned by the hate in my heart and I did not want to allow my hate to conquer my life any longer. I told him I knew I would eventually do something when I got married and had children, and that I would have to seek forgiveness for it, so I wanted to forgive him as I hoped they would forgive me. My father sat on the phone, listening. He did not interrupt. He allowed me to get my comments out. Once I paused as to allow him to speak, he admitted he understood why I felt the way I did. He commended my mother for the great job she did with my brother and me, with the limited resources she had. He acknowledged she is the main reason my brother and I are successful. I told him I appreciated him for saying that, and I agreed.

He continued to tell me he was proud of everything I had accomplished and strived to accomplish. He also said he understood what it meant to have an absent father. That statement caught me off guard. I was under the impression that my father was raised by both of my grandparents, but he told me he left his father's home at age five with his mother. She and my grandfather had split up, and my grandmother had moved my father to Oklahoma City.

As my father was telling me this, I was thinking about the questions I had in my head about why he was in Oklahoma City during his high school years, as my sister and I had been researching his history a few months earlier. He also let me know my grandfather was not an active parent in his life while he was growing up. My father explained that he would leave tickets for my grandfather at his sporting games, but my grandfather would not attend. That statement hit me hard; I felt the same pain from my father because he only attended a couple games during my sports career. My father said he moved back down to Arkansas a few years after he graduated from college so he could build a better relationship with his father. I thought that was special, and it took guts to fight for his relationship with his father. I commended him for that.

I could tell my father was getting choked up a bit when he was talking about my grandfather. The conversation went on for a total of 10 minutes, but I was able to have the most meaningful discussion I have ever had with my father. He opened up about his support for my process of writing this book. I was interested to know that my absent father felt that he had an absent father himself. Although being a child with an absent father is no excuse for becoming an absent father, too, a person cannot help but be compassionate about children who grow up without their fathers in their lives. I was relieved that my father did not yell or get upset with me about this book. Granted, he has not read it yet, so I do not know how he will react after he reads it. Toward the conclusion of the conversation, I mentioned the possibility of his attending speaking engagements with me in the future to share his story. He thought that was a great idea and he welcomed the invitation.

The 10-minute conversation with my father opened my eyes to his feelings and his side of his story. I felt a better connection with him, as we had both come from the same background of having an absent father in our eyes. The choices my father made are ones I hope to learn from so I won't make the same mistakes. He has taught me more by his actions or inactions than he will ever know. My father is human, and we are all sinners. I know he would tell me he does not want any of his children to live the life he did. That is the same statement I would make to my children.

Parents want their children to learn from their mistakes. Some children do, and some children do not. Regardless, I have learned my father's past is behind him, and I hope he continues to try to build a better future with all of his children. The journey for *The Absent Father* is still at its beginning. I have conquered my fear of sharing this story and message with others, and I have become a better person. As this journey continues, I hope I can offer a small glimmer of hope to young people and, adults convincing them if they take small steps, they, too, can forgive and heal themselves and others.

As my grandparents look down on me, I pray I have made them proud. I know my grandfathers, David and Hardy, would have big smiles on their faces, telling me to get out there and make my dreams come true. I know my Nanny and my grandmother would sit me down and reassure me I have a gift that is supposed to be shared with as many people as possible. Finally, my Uncle Billy would look me in my eyes and say, "If you believe you can do it, I am with you 100 percent!" Their prayers have gone a long way toward pushing me forward, and for that I am grateful.

Thank you all for believing in me enough to purchase my book. May all of your dreams come true, and let's spread love, not hate.